Acclaim for
The Ice Sculptures: A Novel of Hollywood

"Liberally laced with sex and sin, *The Ice Sculptures* takes the reader into the world of Hollywood, in which being open and gay can destroy an actor's career—but being closeted and gay can destroy his heart.

In this fun tale by Michael D. Craig, actor Tim Race rises from the modest beginnings to action-movie superstardom all the while enjoying the willing and available men around him. But just as the ice sculptures of the title, Tim's life is perfect, yet cold.

The author takes us behind the scenes of Hollywood sets, Hollywood homes, and Hollywood sex with an insider's authority and knowledge. Tim Race crisscrosses the world as he becomes more and more famous, always with three close friends to keep him grounded. But when Tim falls for a young man, he must decide between his career and his heart. And, just as in real life, Michael Craig deftly shows us that both coming out of and staying in the closet have their price."

—Jonathan Cohen
Author of *Bear Like Me*

"Fast paced and easy to read, *The Ice Sculptures* reconstitutes the world in which movie studios covered up the indiscretions of their stars. It provides an escape from the tell-all celebrity world of today to Jacqueline Susann's world of dark secrets and designer labels—but with twenty-first century sex."

—Edmund Miller, PhD
ht Times

"Author Michael D. Craig has crea   heart-
throb in Tim Race. *The Ice Sculptu*   way to
spend an afternoon."

—Dale Edgerton
Author of *Goneaway Road*

The Ice Sculptures
A Novel of Hollywood

HARRINGTON PARK PRESS

Southern Tier Editions
Gay Men's Fiction
Jay Quinn, Executive Editor

This Thing Called Courage: South Boston Stories by J. G. Hayes

Trio Sonata by Juliet Sarkessian

Bear Like Me by Jonathan Cohen

Ambidextrous: The Secret Lives of Children by Felice Picano

Men Who Loved Me by Felice Picano

A House on the Ocean, A House on the Bay by Felice Picano

Goneaway Road by Dale Edgerton

Death Trick: A Murder Mystery by Richard Stevenson

The Concrete Sky by Marshall Moore

Edge by Jeff Mann

Through It Came Bright Colors by Trebor Healey

Elf Child by David M. Pierce

Huddle by Dan Boyle

The Man Pilot by James W. Ridout IV

Shadows of the Night: Queer Tales of the Uncanny and Unusual edited by Greg Herren

Van Allen's Ecstasy by Jim Tushinski

Beyond the Wind by Rob N. Hood

The Handsomest Man in the World by David Leddick

The Song of a Manchild by Durrell Owens

The Ice Sculptures: A Novel of Hollywood by Michael D. Craig

Between the Palms: A Collection of Gay Travel Erotica by Michael T. Luongo

Aura by Gary Glickman

Love Under Foot: An Erotic Celebration of Feet by Greg Wharton and M. Christian

The Tenth Man by E. William Podojil

Upon a Midnight Clear: Queer Christmas Tales edited by Greg Herren

Dryland's End by Felice Picano

Whose Eye Is on Which Sparrow? by Robert Taylor

The Ice Sculptures
A Novel of Hollywood

Michael D. Craig

Southern Tier Editions
Harrington Park Press®
An Imprint of The Haworth Press, Inc.
New York • London • Oxford

Published by

Southern Tier Editions, Harrington Park Press®, an imprint of The Haworth Press, Inc., 10 Alice Street, Binghamton, NY 13904-1580.

PUBLISHER'S NOTE
This is a work of fiction. Names, characters, places, and incidents either are the products of the author's imagination or are used fictitiously, and any resemblance to actual persons, living or dead, business establishments, events, or locales is entirely coincidental.

Cover design by Marylouise E. Doyle.

Library of Congress Cataloging-in-Publication Data

Craig, Michael D.
  The ice sculptures : a novel of Hollywood / Michael D. Craig.
    p. cm.
  ISBN 1-56023-481-4 (soft : alk. paper)
  1. Motion picture actors and actresses—Fiction. 2. Hollywood (Los Angeles, Calif.)—Fiction.
3. Passing (Identity)—Fiction. 4. Gay men—-Fiction. I. Title.
PS3603.R355128 2004
813'.6—dc22
                                                                          2003017951

for **M.M.,**
the love of my life—of a hundred lifetimes—if you only knew.
My love for you is forever.

And for the real **Jaime Adame.**
May you have found happiness and love,
wherever in this world you may be.

The Ice Sculptures

Carved from ice with the greatest of skill,
Beautiful to behold, a shimmer of a thrill.
Glistening in the sun for a brief moment in time,
Melting away, drop by drop, long before their prime.

A masterpiece of splendid creation,
Etched in the cold and brought to fruition.
So quickly they pass, dissolving away,
Not meant to survive for another day.

The Ice Sculptures stand alone, fragile to the touch
Translucent and ephemeral, their beauty a crutch.
For time moves forward without a single pause,
Leaving behind, in its wake, everything that was . . .

Prologue   Hollywood, California

He had imagined this moment countless times over the years. The reality of it, however, was far greater than anything he had ever envisioned while growing up in a small and dusty Texas town. The long and perilous ride to this point had been worth it. Certainly sacrifices had been made along the way, but there were always sacrifices to be made in life.

The charcoal-gray limousine pulled to a stop in front of the Shrine Auditorium, which resembled a tacky Hollywood version of the Taj Mahal, with its whitewashed, onion-shaped domes reflecting the bright light of the sun. This would be the last time the outdated venue would host the Academy Awards, as the glitzy and modern new Kodak Theatre was nearing completion close by on Hollywood Boulevard and Highland Avenue. Timothy glanced over at his companion, Raina Hawthorne. She looked so beautiful, so glamorous in her lavender Escada gown with the scalloped hemline, a stylishly diaphanous organza wrap covering her bare arms. The spectacular $3.5 million diamond and amethyst necklace on loan from Bulgari sparkled enticingly from her flawless décolletage. A matching set of earrings dangled from her petite ears. The necklace and earrings had been sent by courier from the world-famous jeweler's flagship store in Rome, accompanied by two burly bodyguards.

She is indeed one of the world's most stunning women, Tim thought as he stared at her radiant beauty. Millions of men the world over would kill to be in his place right now. Often, when he was alone in his bed at night, he would think of her magnificent face and body. He would wish that he could long for it, could feel a passion and desire to hold her next to his body and make love to her with an abandon he had never felt. Life would be so much simpler for him if only he could.

1

Raina looked over at him, her violet eyes twinkling in the dim light that filtered through the tinted windows of the limousine. She smiled nervously and tugged on her bottom lip with her pearly white teeth.

"Well, this is it. Time to put on a show for the entire world to see." She had taken out a lighted compact to inspect her face and hair one last time. Her naturally blonde and curly hair had been straightened for the event, and against her forehead were draped several lustrous tendrils, which she expertly brushed away from her eyes with a well-manicured hand. She placed the compact back into her one-of-a-kind Judith Lieber purse, the shape and color of a ripe plum, before making sure the straps on her Manolo Blahnik sandals were in place. She rarely wore high heels while in Tim's company, as they made her tower over him like an Amazon. The purse and shoes had been a gift from Tim, just to show his appreciation for all of her years of support and friendship.

"I'm ready if you are," he replied in the low, husky voice that was famous throughout the entire world.

"Let's do it then," she said with a wink, reaching over to straighten the bow tie on his Versace tuxedo that perfectly matched the silk fabric of her evening gown.

The back door to the limousine was opened by the liveried chauffeur, and the flash of a thousand cameras added to the bright sunlight outside, causing them both to squint as they exited the limousine. The two Roman bodyguards, who had been following in a separate car, immediately flanked them.

"What will you do if you win the Oscar tonight?" Raina whispered softly into his ear as they faced the crowd, the clicks from the cameras reaching a feverish pitch. Hundreds of people were shouting out their names, desperate to catch their attention, however briefly.

"That stuffy old Academy would never give me the Oscar. I haven't paid my dues in this town yet," he commented wryly.

"You've given away more of yourself than any actor I've ever known," Raina said through her smile. The couple made the obligatory 360-degree turn on the red carpet so they could be photographed from every angle.

"Sometimes you have to make the ultimate sacrifice to get ahead in this town."

"I believe you are right, my dear. Hollywood cannibalizes the very people it wishes to admire," Raina replied, still smiling broadly for the cameras.

They passed an impressive ice sculpture on their way to meet the throng of television reporters, photographers, and journalists hungrily awaiting their arrival. The sculpture was over six feet tall and skillfully carved to resemble an Oscar statuette. It was beginning to melt in the warmth of the Southern California sun, and a small puddle of water had formed around the base. Tim thought how sad it was that someone had spent so much time creating something so beautiful, only to have it melt away a few hours later.

The sound of the crowd suddenly grew more intense. Tim stopped walking midstep. The camera flashes continued, along with the cheers from the crowd. All of his life, this was the very moment he had anticipated, dreamed about, fought so hard to achieve. They were calling his name. They loved him. They wanted him. He had never felt happier in his entire life.

BOOK ONE:
A MAP TO THE STARS

Tim placed the Steppenwolf CD into the console and turned up the volume. "Born to Be Wild" seemed like the appropriate listening material under the circumstances. The engine of his brand-new, jet-black Mercedes-Benz SLK 320 convertible purred contentedly as he sped along the desolate highway. He tapped the steering wheel to the beat of the music and felt the sweet euphoria of freedom. He had been trapped in that antiseptic clinic for almost a week. It felt as if he had been there twice as long. It just wasn't for him. Too many doctors and nurses who felt they knew exactly what he was going through. Too many catatonic patients wandering the halls looking as if they were going to lose their tenuous grasps on sanity at any given moment. He didn't need any of that. He didn't have a problem, after all, at least not anything that he couldn't take care of himself.

The song came to an end and he ejected the CD. He tried tuning in a radio station but there was no reception in the middle of the desert, only the monotonous whir of static. Tim switched the radio off and breathed in the air. Fresh and dry. You could never breathe air like this in Los Angeles. Good thing he wasn't a smoker; then he would really be in trouble. Emphysema wasn't a pretty way to go. His grandfather had died of emphysema. A vision of his Grandpa Tully popped into his mind. His grandfather was the only member of his family that he truly missed. Suddenly, memories of the person he had been before and all of the things he had endured to reach this point in his life began to fill his mind.

Had that boy from a small Texas town ever really existed?

He had not spoken with his father Carl in years, not since he had made his acting debut on the television soap opera *The Drifting Clouds* many years before. His father didn't agree with his lifestyle, living in "Hollyweird," as he referred to LA, a town full of faggots, crackheads, and two-bit hookers. Dad had been raised a God-fearing Southern

Baptist and he had instilled that same fear in his only child. His mother, Deanna, had been meek and submissive and had allowed his father to bully both of them mercilessly throughout his childhood. Tim had become accustomed to his father's taunts and jeers over the years, the way he called him a sissy and a queer. He had responded by working out with weights to build up his body and joining the local football team. His father was unimpressed. On the football field, he was strong and in command. No one would have dared call him names, as there was an intensity in his emerald green eyes that cautioned people not to mess with him.

As Tim drove the Mercedes along the lonely highway, speeding toward San Diego, he had time to think of his life and everything he had experienced over the past decade. He was *the* Tim Race, the macho box office god whose films could do no wrong. He was thirty-one years old and at the top of his form. He had an Oscar and a Golden Globe to his credit. He earned a staggering $20 million per picture. His palatial home in Bel Air had made the cover of *Architectural Digest*. Beautiful people of both sexes were continually throwing themselves at his feet. It was far more than he ever could have imagined. So, where did everything go wrong? Why did he just break out of the Salvation Drug and Alcohol Treatment Center in Palm Desert, to which the studio was paying more than $10,000 a week to treat his so-called addictions?

Drugs had never been Tim's scene. Last year, shortly before the Academy Awards, he had gone for a routine dentist appointment. The dentist informed him that his wisdom teeth had impacted and needed to be removed. He had always had a raving phobia about dentists and their drills, and now he was suffering the consequences. It was bad timing, of course, but what could be done? The doctor had prescribed him Vicodin for the pain, but Tim had been a baby with a low pain threshold and asked the dentist to up the dosage. That had been a mistake.

Then there was the acrimonious breakup with David. He still could not believe it was over. They had been so in love. Sure, there had been others, and Tim knew that David also had the occasional dalliance with one of his young, gorgeous male clients. What was that old

Tinseltown adage? *Doesn't count on location.* They both lived in Hollywood, after all. But they had been together for almost eleven years,
which was a lifetime by LA standards. It wasn't as if they could have
lived together openly in a loving relationship. That would have been
poison to Tim's magnificent career. America expected Tim Race to be
a paragon of heterosexuality. Hollywood could say that gays had a
place in their world. They could point out Rupert Everett, an openly
homosexual man, and his leap from supporting actor to headlining
star. They could make mention of myriad gay characters currently
populating television sitcoms and dramas. Everyone knew that it was
just lip service. An actor who lived openly as a homosexual would
never be the top-rated box office draw in the world.

When he was awarded the Oscar for his universally acclaimed performance in *Weak Are the Kind,* it had been the pinnacle of his career.
The studio had initially offered the role to Tom Hanks, who had been
too busy to commit. Then to Travolta, who passed. Nicolas Cage had
expressed an interest, as had Brad Pitt and Ben Affleck. Tim began to
campaign for the role with a mad passion immediately after reading
the Pulitzer Prize–winning novel upon which the movie was to be
based. Tim had wanted the role of the hopeless alcoholic so badly he
could taste it. He told David to let the studio know he would take a
massive pay cut in order to do the film; he was even willing to work
for scale. David had tried to dissuade him from accepting the role, as it
was a far cry from the action films that had made him an international
superstar. But Tim had been adamant. He knew when he read the
script that it was a role of a lifetime, and he had been right.

When the studio cast Raina Hawthorne to play his long-suffering
wife in the film, it had been kismet. Raina had advanced far from her
role on a popular, lowbrow sitcom to become one of the sexiest and
most bankable female stars in Hollywood. They had met years earlier
and had become great friends. Raina knew Tim's little secret and had
gladly accepted the role of his beard to protect it. She was thrilled
when he won the Academy Award, and he had thanked her lovingly
in a moving acceptance speech that left the audience in tears. Raina
had beamed with great pride that night, even though everyone in
town knew that she had been robbed of a nomination for her own

amazing performance in the film. Raina was a rarity in Hollywood: a kind, generous, and supremely talented actress with a breathtaking natural beauty, untouched by the plastic surgeon's scalpel.

There were always the rumors, of course, low and persistent. Tim imagined it to be a sort of parlor game in homes across America: Was he or wasn't he gay? To circumvent the rumors, Raina and Tim made sure to be photographed together at least once a month. There was the vacation to Sardinia, where the two had been invited to cruise the Mediterranean on the luxurious yacht belonging to a wealthy European businessman. Photographs frequently appeared in *People* and *Star* magazines showing Tim and Raina strolling along Madison Avenue in New York or at the Beverly Center in LA, holding hands and enjoying a day of leisurely shopping. There were the photographs of the pair attending the Kentucky Derby at Churchill Downs on the first Saturday in May, Tim wearing an ascot and dark sunglasses and Raina wearing an outlandish hat, both drinking mint juleps while seated with the other famous faces on Millionaires' Row. Not to mention the endless movie premieres and awards shows the two dutifully attended together. Sometimes David would tag along. It did not look suspicious, as David was both Tim and Raina's agent. He always lurked in the background, careful not to be photographed very often with Tim.

Tim thought about David: kind, wonderful, amazing David. He couldn't imagine loving anyone else. What had happened between them? Then Tim remembered. He had broken the cardinal rule, the unwritten show biz caveat: *Never bring your lover home.* Tim had met the cute blond at the Ivy restaurant in Santa Monica. He had been having lunch alone at an intimate table on the patio, eating a plate of the famous Ivy grilled vegetable salad, when the muscular and tanned young man had approached him, notebook in hand, smiling a killer smile and politely asking for Tim's autograph. Tim scrawled his name on the paper and added a little note: *Meet me outside in fifteen minutes. Be alone.*

It had all been so spontaneous, just a quick and immediate release from the tensions and stress of his busy Hollywood career. The sexy young thing had followed him in his car to his gated home in Bel Air.

There had been no preamble. It was just hot, delicious, uncomplicated sex. Things did not remain uncomplicated, however. David had arrived at the house. The studio had called him at his Malibu home, inquiring about Tim's location. He was supposed to have shown up for a line reading with potential costars for his upcoming movie, *A Mission from Hell.* Tim and the muscular blond did not hear David when he entered the bedroom.

Tim had never seen David so furious. The passion had gone from their sex life and now he was turning to *trade* to satisfy his desires, David had raged, veins bulging in his neck. Tim had felt like a sack of shit. David then announced that he would no longer be Tim's agent. He stormed from the house, and they hadn't spoken since.

That was when he started to take more pills. At first, the dentist had been reluctant to prescribe him more Vicodin. It was a powerful narcotic, after all. Tim told him that his mouth still had not healed properly from the oral surgery and that he was in constant pain. The doctor relented and gave him the refill. First one refill, then two and three. Soon, Tim couldn't make it through the day without ingesting a handful of the white, egg-shaped pills. He began to show up late on the set of *A Mission from Hell.* He had trouble remembering his lines. He would lose his balance during crucial action scenes. Then his looks began to suffer. He lost a considerable amount of weight. The role required an actor of a certain weight and physical stature. One of the British rags alleged that he was HIV positive, claiming to have received the information from Tim's personal physician. The story was later retracted after his attorneys threatened litigation. There were murmurs that the movie was in trouble. *Variety* reported that the film was millions of dollars over budget. Finally, it was announced that Tim Race had to withdraw from production for unspecified personal reasons.

The tabloids and press had a field day. "Tim Race in Drug-Induced Rage" shouted *The Globe.* "Race's Multimillion-Dollar Addiction" proclaimed *The National Enquirer.* It was the lead story on *Entertainment Tonight* and *Access Hollywood* for one week straight. An article appeared in *The New York Times* suggesting he was the latest victim of the infamous "Oscar Curse" that had plagued winners since the award's inception. Tim was actually amused by it all, as at least they were not speculating on his sexual proclivities.

Then the studio issued an ultimatum. He could either enter a treatment center or it would sue him for breach of contract. The studio was investing millions of dollars in the movie and was not about to have its most popular star throw it all away.

Tim had finally relented and agreed to enter treatment. That had been a week ago. And now he was on the lam from the Salvation Drug and Alcohol Treatment Center in Palm Desert, California, and from an angry studio that had blown $30 million on a film it could not finish without its leading man.

Ahead of him, the sun was setting low on the horizon. He approached a sign that read SAN DIEGO NEXT TWELVE EXITS. He slowed the Mercedes and pulled onto the first off-ramp. It had been a while since he had been in San Diego. He always enjoyed himself whenever he was in town. Surely, there would be something for him to do.

Then the question popped into his mind again: *Had that boy from a small Texas town ever really existed?*

He had plotted his great escape from Tenpole, Texas, for years. He knew where he needed to be in the world. There was only one place for him, really. The crudely written tales about Los Angeles in the back pages of his mother's copies of *True Story* and *Hollywood Confidential* had always enticed him. Sure, there were lurid stories of sex, drugs, and murder but also tales of actors who had come from nowhere and started with nothing and turned themselves into celebrated stars—icons such as James Dean, Paul Newman, Steve McQueen, and Robert Mitchum. He was certain he could do the same for himself. One day Timothy Gividend was going to be famous. He had two things going for him: a burning ambition to succeed in life and a gorgeous face and body. He had squirreled away all of the money he had earned from pumping gas at the local Texaco station in a coffee can he hid in the stump of an old oak tree on his grandfather's cattle ranch. There was also the money his Grandpa Tully had given him for helping with the crops and taking care of his farm once he became too ill to work. It wasn't much, but at least it would get him to where he needed to be.

The day after he graduated valedictorian from high school, the class of 1989, he packed up his belongings and hitched a ride into town to catch a bus to Los Angeles. There had been offers from colleges, universities with excellent football programs trying to woo him to attend their schools, but he knew that college was not going to get him to where he wanted to be in life. He had told his mother he was leaving that morning, once his father had left early for work in one of the many oil fields that dotted the Texas plain. She had cried, begging him to stay. She couldn't face the days without her only son, she said. Tim suspected that what she feared the most was being left alone with his father. He had been detached and emotionless with her, wishing her well and thanking her for helping raise him into the world, a world he was now venturing out into, not knowing what it held in store for him.

He experienced his first sexual encounter on the dusty bus trip across the Texas panhandle. There was a smattering of people on the bus, sweaty and unsmiling faces anxious to end their trips and to escape the unbearable heat. He had noticed the older man in the gray slacks eyeing him when he first got on the bus in Tenpole. Tim acknowledged him with a nod of the head and then immediately removed the shopworn Robert Ludlum paperback from his duffel bag and began to read. There were few distractions on the bus, only the stranger turning around to look at him from time to time and the low cries and gurgles of a baby belonging to a teenaged mother seated near the front of the bus.

By the time the bus made its first stop an hour and a half later, the man in the gray slacks had moved to the seat across the aisle from Tim. He made small talk, commenting about the insufferable heat and informing Tim that Robert Ludlum was his favorite novelist of all time. The man told him that his name was Rich and that he was from Tulsa and was traveling to Phoenix to visit a sick relative. Tim nodded politely every few minutes and answered the man's questions but was careful not to reveal too much of himself. They were the only passengers on the bus engaging in any sort of conversation, as by now most everyone else was asleep, except for a blue-haired elderly woman in the front seat behind the driver, who was busily knitting a bright yellow scarf.

The bus pulled into a tiny station in a nameless, one-stop-sign town somewhere near the New Mexico border. The bus driver informed them that they would be there awhile to refuel and added that they were almost a half hour ahead of schedule. Tim got off the bus to stretch his legs and take a piss. A few other passengers also left the bus to buy a cold drink and to take a break from the stifling heat. Tim strolled into the station and asked the attendant where the bathrooms were located. The old man looked up from the newspaper he was reading and pointed a bony finger toward the back of the room. Tim passed several rows of overpriced junk food and outdated magazines and entered the bathroom. The door had the word "Gentlemen" scrawled on it in black marker. He stood before the urinal and unzipped his pants. He took in a deep breath and held it to avoid the overpowering ammonia scent that emanated from the urinal, which looked as if it hadn't been cleaned in months. A cockroach scurried beneath his feet. From behind him, he heard the door slowly creak open. He glanced in the mirror above the washbasin and saw the man from the bus. He looked directly into Tim's eyes and held his gaze for a moment. Tim looked down and tapped his penis lightly to rid it of any droplets of urine. The man's breath was heavy in the silence of the room.

Tim turned around and faced the man. Rich was now staring at the obvious bulge that had formed in Tim's pants. No words were exchanged between them. It was an unspoken language, a language Tim understood instinctively. He had known what the man wanted the moment he had gotten onto the bus in Tenpole. Tim had wanted it too. The stranger slid the flimsy chain lock on the bathroom door into place to prevent them from being disturbed. Slowly, the man reached down and unzipped Tim's jeans completely, fumbling with his black leather belt. He grabbed Tim's turgid cock and expertly masturbated him, making it grow harder in his hand. Tim thought that the man's hands were surprisingly soft and tender, without the calluses caused by hard labor. Rich knelt down before him and lifted up Tim's polo shirt slightly to massage the tight, flat muscles of his tanned stomach. Tim breathed out a long sigh and leaned back against the washbasin. When Rich took Tim's penis into his mouth, a low growl formed in the back of Tim's throat. Tim began to stroke the man's hair. It felt like crushed velvet between his fingers and was the color of freshly ground ginger as it glistened in the harsh light from the bathroom's bare bulb. It was sweet and immediate release. The man quickened the pace, and Tim leaned back harder against the washbasin, his knees buckling as he arched his back upward to meet the warm embrace of the man's eager mouth. He felt no shame or worries, as he was far away from his disapproving father and the narrow-minded people of Tenpole, Texas. When he came, he let out a surprised gasp at the intensity of his orgasm. Endorphins coursed throughout his body and a thousand brilliant colors flashed across his mind.

It was sweet and immediate release.

When the feeling of euphoria had finally ebbed from his body, Tim zipped up his pants and turned immediately to the washbasin, cleaning his hands with the amber-colored antibacterial soap and splashing cold water across his flushed face. He looked into his own eyes in the cracked and spotted mirror. It felt as if he was truly looking at himself for the first time in all of his eighteen years of life. He finally knew his true identity in this world. The man coughed slightly to clear his throat. Tim stepped aside and allowed him to wash up. Tim watched silently as Rich removed a rough, brown paper towel from the dispenser and wiped his face clean. As he exited the bathroom, he gave Tim a wink.

Five minutes later everyone had boarded the bus. The bus left the lonely station behind in the dark. Tim and the stranger did not speak for the rest of the trip. As the man got off the bus at his stop outside of Phoenix, he patted Tim lightly on the shoulder and gave him a knowing smile. Tim smiled back. Then he closed his eyes and slept peacefully the rest of the way to Los Angeles.

That first week in LA had been intimidating. He had only enough money to stay in a seedy motel in West Hollywood, a section of the city Tim had heard was very open to gay men. He spent most of his days pounding the beat, searching for a job. Unfortunately, most places of business were not eager to hire a newcomer to the area, especially someone with limited work experience and no permanent residence. He was beginning to feel depressed when one day he was approached by a handsome, older man with a Vandyke goatee as he walked by the motel's pool. He was the owner of the motel and was in a pinch because his super had gotten busted for crack cocaine possession and had been hauled off to jail. He commented that Tim looked like he was handy with a hammer and offered him the job. It didn't pay much, but he could stay at the motel for free. Tim readily accepted the man's offer and they shook hands.

Soon enough, Tim was being run ragged by his new boss, Simon. There was always something to fix or an errand to run. Simon had given him a beat-up old Ford pickup to drive around the city. Within a few weeks, Tim was comfortable in his new surroundings.

The months passed by without any noticeable changing of the seasons. At Christmastime, he had called home to speak to his mother. Her voice had been warm and loving over the phone. She hoped that he was happy in his new life and that he would one day learn to forgive her for not being a better mother to him. She told him that his father missed him as well, but Tim did not really believe her. He was probably glad to be rid of his sissy of a son. Tim had wished his mother a merry Christmas and hung up the phone. He was spending Christmas alone in his room at the motel. He had made a few friends, mostly other employees at the motel. Simon had invited him to spend Christmas Eve with his wife and children at his house in the Valley, but Tim had declined the invitation. He didn't feel much like celebrating Christmas, and he was beginning to wonder if his dreams of becoming famous would ever come true.

It was a warm late-spring day when something happened that would alter Tim's life forever. He had been on an errand for Simon that took him through the swanky part of the city. After picking up a delivery, he drove past the flashy storefronts of Rodeo Drive. He marveled at the luxurious goods the stores and boutiques offered. Driving the battered pickup truck, he felt out of place among the chauffeur-driven Rolls-Royces and Bentleys, with their occupants hidden behind smoky glass windows, and men in $4,000 suits talking on cell phones as they expertly navigated their BMWs through the crowded streets. It all seemed to him like something out of a gaudy Jackie Collins novel.

Suddenly, there was a quick jolt and a loud crashing noise. He had just rear-ended the car in front of him! He cursed at himself loudly as he pulled off the side of the road behind the shiny red BMW with the now-damaged bumper. Tim couldn't believe his carelessness. He was always such a considerate driver, one of the few things his father had taught him to be.

The door to the BMW opened and a tall, lean man who appeared to be in his early thirties got out of the car, a mobile phone in his hand. Tim expected the man to be belligerent, but he was smiling as he approached the truck.

"Hello. It appears we've had a little accident here," he said with a smile as he lifted his Ray-Ban sunglasses to reveal sparkling blue eyes. His teeth were a gleaming white and perfectly aligned in his mouth, his lips full and rich and a shade of deepest burgundy. His face was evenly tanned and his complexion, smooth and unwrinkled, perfectly complemented his honey-blond hair. Tim felt his heart skip a beat.

The man was staring at him, expecting him to respond. When Tim didn't, he continued, "I really should have been paying more attention to what I was doing. I was on the phone fussing at my secretary about a contract that was supposed to be written up and signed and I didn't see the stoplight until it was almost too late. I'm David Reardon, by the way." He extended his hand through the window of the truck for Tim to shake.

When Tim again failed to respond, he said, "And you are?"

Tim felt his face grow hot. "I—I'm sorry," he stammered as he shook the man's hand. "My name is Timothy Gividend."

"Nice to meet you, Timothy," David replied. "I'd better call the police. Of course, it might take them a while to respond in this town. The LAPD aren't exactly known for their efficiency." He laughed and Tim smiled back at him.

"So, Tim, what do you do for a living?" he asked after he had telephoned the police. Tim got out of the truck to inspect the damage to both vehicles. The truck's grill was only slightly damaged, but the back end of the BMW was smashed in considerably. "Let me guess. You're an actor?"

"Not really," Tim said, feeling himself blush again.

"Then that must mean you are an unemployed actor. There are quite a few of those in this town. Have you done anything that I would have seen or heard about?" he queried.

Tim shook his head. "The only thing I've ever been in are a few plays in high school."

"Don't knock it. That's how half of the big-name stars in this town got their starts. I guess I should tell you that I'm an agent and I represent some up-and-coming talent." He reached into the pocket of his blue Armani suit and pulled out a business card, which he then handed to Tim.

"You're really an agent?" Tim asked in surprise, inspecting the small beige card with bright red lettering that read REARDON & BORSTEIN TALENT AGENCY.

"Indeed I am. I suppose it can only be official once you have business cards printed up with your name on them. You know, you have a very handsome face, if you don't mind me saying so. A very nice build as well. Good smile, perfect hair. I might be able to find you some work, if you would be interested."

"Are you kidding? I would be more than interested. I've dreamed of being an actor since I was a little boy growing up in Texas."

"Texas boy, huh? I hear they grow 'em big in Texas," he said jokingly, emphasizing the word *big* while eyeing Tim's muscular physique once again.

Tim smiled back at David sheepishly. Just then, a police cruiser pulled up to break the moment.

It took a half hour to fill out the accident report. After the brawny and unfriendly police officer had returned to his cruiser, David asked Tim if he wanted to come over to his home in the Malibu Colony to talk about acting possibilities. He told Tim he couldn't make any promises in regard to representing him as his agent. Tim nodded and said that was all right with him; he was appreciative that David would even consider being his agent.

Tim followed behind the damaged BMW, ecstatic at this incredible stroke of luck. They soon arrived at David's magnificent Malibu beach house. Tim's jaw dropped in amazement.

"Do you like the house?" David asked unnecessarily; he could tell by the expression on Tim's face that he was very impressed.

The interior of the home was equally stunning. It was designed as a two-story loft with a spiral staircase leading up to the second level.

The front of the house was an enormous bay window that looked out onto the broad expanse of the Pacific Ocean. The sparkling white sand of Malibu Beach glowed in the sun and was dotted with people enjoying the surf and the beauty of their surroundings.

Tim asked if he could borrow the phone so that he could call his boss and let him know about the accident and that he would be late returning to the motel. After informing Simon that the truck had not been seriously damaged, he hung up and turned to look out at the ocean. He heard David whistling as he descended the spiral staircase. Tim turned to face him. He had changed from his pressed Armani suit to khaki shorts and a blue-and-white-striped pullover shirt. His bare feet moved noiselessly across the coolness of the stark white floor tiles. Tim stared at him, feeling the familiar clutch in his chest.

"I think I might have a job for you," he said after he offered Tim a drink from the fully stocked wet bar. Tim accepted a frosty mug of Corona beer that David kept on tap. They were now sitting in the living room on the expensive leather sofa that faced the beach.

"Really? What kind of a job?" Tim asked excitedly, although he was secretly wondering if this guy was on the up-and-up.

"It's nothing all that impressive. A soap company is looking for a good-looking young guy like you to appear in a commercial for their newest deodorant bar. It would require you to take your shirt off. That's not a problem for you, is it?"

"Heck, no," Tim replied.

"Good. You wouldn't be required to speak, unfortunately. They will hire someone else to do a voice-over. You just have to look sexy. Think you can handle that?"

"Not a problem," Tim responded confidently.

"Of course, I'd have to see what you look like under those clothes, to make sure you have the look the company is searching for, you understand."

"That's cool. Do you want me to take my shirt off for you?"

David nodded. Tim wasted no time in pulling his T-shirt over his head and tossing it gently across the back of the sofa.

David's blue eyes seemed to darken a shade as he examined Tim's muscular, hairless torso, his tongue pressed firmly against the back of

his teeth. "Very nice, indeed. You obviously work out a great deal."
Tim nodded as he did a quick turn so David could examine his back as
well. "Yes, I think you will do quite nicely. Of course, you'll have to
get your SAG card before you can work. That's the Screen Actors
Guild. It shouldn't be a problem. I can pull some strings."

David took another sip of the sherry he had poured for himself and
placed the Waterford crystal glass carefully on a coaster on the glass
coffee table. "So, do we have a deal? Do you want to be represented by
the Reardon and Borstein Talent Agency?"

"If you'll have me as a client, I'm all yours," Tim said ebulliently.

David clapped his hands together. "Fantastic! Let me get out a contract for you to sign, to make it official." He stood up, walked over to
a mahogany desk, and opened up a drawer to pull out the paperwork.
"There's a lot of legalese in the contract, so don't let that scare you.
It's a standard industry contract, stating that I get fifteen percent of
whatever you earn from any acting jobs my agency secures for you. If
you would feel more comfortable, you could have a lawyer look it over
to make sure it's kosher."

Tim shook his head. "No need for that. I trust you. I don't want to
waste any time or money with lawyers. Just show me where I have to
sign."

David's eyes sparkled brightly. He grabbed a $300 Montblanc pen
from the pencil holder on his desk and handed it to Tim. Tim placed
the contract on the desk and signed his name with a flourish on the
line David had indicated.

"Welcome aboard, Timothy Gividend. Let's hope we have a long
and prosperous relationship."

They both returned to the sofa and grabbed their drinks from the
coffee table for a toast. The sunlight from the massive bay window
cast dancing shadows across Tim's bare chest.

"My God, but you are beautiful," David half-whispered as he finished off the last of the sherry in his glass.

A tingling sensation began in Tim's chest and filtered throughout
the rest of his body. He hadn't had sex since the stranger in the bus
station. Some older men who stayed at the motel and hung around
the pool had expressed interest in him. He had been in search of some-

thing else. He boldly moved closer to David on the sofa and took David's hand in both of his. He placed David's hand on his own chest, between the chiseled hardness of his pectoral muscles that flinched under the electric spark from David's touch. David breathed out an almost inaudible sigh as he moved his face toward Tim's. Their lips parted softly as they kissed, both of them drinking in the delirium of their sudden burst of passion. A collision of tongues was quickly followed by ardent caresses, hands moving swiftly across bare flesh and restrictive clothing. Soon, the clothing was gone, tossed haphazardly across the white tiled floor and the expensive furniture.

David was going to be Tim's teacher. He was experienced and could show Tim all of the little tricks that only someone who'd tasted the finer things in life would know. He was also Tim's key to the life that he had always wanted for himself. He willingly submitted to David's expert attention. The older man touched him on every part of his lithe body, taunting and teasing him onward, being aggressive one moment and submissive the next. David extracted a condom from a nearby drawer and gingerly placed it on Tim's penis. He showed Tim how to warm him up, to prepare for the penetration that was to come. Tim reveled in the dark and mysterious taste of him, making David beg for more. There were exotic oils to choose from as well, oils of varying hues, scents, and flavors. David covered Tim's fingers in a clear, lightly scented oil and slowly placed Tim's two lubricated digits inside his own rectum, causing him to moan intensely.

He was ready for Tim now. David guided him inside as he leaned forward against the soft pillows of the sofa, reaching behind and holding Tim firmly by the buttocks with both of his hands to lock him into place. Tim thrust ahead, slowly at first, not sure exactly how much David could take. David reassured him that everything was fine by pressing harder against him. Tim took his cues from David, monitoring his movements, the sound of his breathing, and the changing tone of his moans and shouts. Tim moaned and shouted as well, their cries forming a chorus, as Tim enjoyed the silky sheath of pleasure that David willingly offered up to him. Tim felt the burning sensation begin deep within his groin, slowly radiating out from the center of his being until it took control of his entire body. He gripped David's hips harshly and pulled his quivering body mercilessly toward him until the burning sensation shattered into a thousand pieces throughout his body.

They both sat on the floor afterward, as the light of day turned into the soft twinkle of twilight. They held each other, still naked and in no hurry to put their clothing on again.

"You were truly spectacular, you know," David murmured into Tim's ear.

"Do you think?" Tim said jokingly as he kissed him lightly on the nape of his neck.

"I really believe you are going to be a big star in this town. I have a sixth sense when it comes to this sort of thing," David told him later as they were both putting on their clothes. Simon had probably called the police by now to report the truck stolen, and Tim had to get back to the motel.

"So, you were serious about the soap commercial?"

"You were thinking maybe I was just leading you on to get into your pants?"

"The thought had occurred to me," Tim responded truthfully.

"No. I would never do something like that to you. Especially not after what we just did together. I will call the April Showers people in the morning to let them know I have their man."

David had been true to his word. Three weeks later, Tim was on the set of his first nationwide television commercial. He had given Simon his notice the week before, and Simon had wished him the best of luck. David had picked Tim up at the motel to drive him to the studio in Burbank where the commercial was to be filmed. David was driving his alternate set of wheels: a vintage, candy-apple red '68 Mustang he had just bought the day before. Tim was nervous on the drive to the studio, but David told him that everything was going to be perfect. He had met with the two men that worked for the April Showers deodorant bar company in David's luxurious Century City offices on the Avenue of the Stars the day before. They had flown in from corporate headquarters in Springfield, Illinois. The two middle-aged men in almost-identical brown suits and blue ties had seemed rather humorless to Tim. They both agreed that Tim had the perfect, all-American look that the company was looking for to represent its product to the nation. Tim didn't have to speak; he only had to flash his magnetic smile and look drop-dead gorgeous, something he did effortlessly. Another contract was produced for Tim to sign, and his heart jumped into his throat when he saw the amount of money they were willing to pay him: $4,500 plus residuals, minus David's 15 percent commission, of course.

Tim was excited as they entered the gates to the studio. The security guard recognized David and waved them through. The thrill of what was happening to him finally began to settle in, and his palms turned moist with nervousness.

Both Hugh and Bob from April Showers were waiting for them in Studio 3D, wearing the same suits from the day before. They appeared to be in a better state of humor, smiling when Tim and David approached them. An attractive older woman with upswept silver hair and horn-rimmed glasses was standing with them. She came over to greet David and Tim.

"There you are, David," she said in a deep Queens accent. "And this must be the hunk?" She smiled at Tim. "I'm Ruth Borstein, my dear, David's not-so-silent partner in the agency." She shook Tim's hand warmly. "So, are you ready to have all of America see your sexy body on TV?"

"Ready as I'll ever be," Tim replied with a smile, immediately taking a liking to Ruth. He could tell from her appearance and demeanor that she was quite the character.

Within minutes, the set was hopping with makeup artists and hairstylists, camera people and members of the lighting crew. Others were busily making up the set, which consisted of a simple tiled shower with a gold-accented faucet and showerhead and a clear vinyl shower curtain. A woman wearing a headset and mouthpiece brought Tim a medium-sized black Speedo and told him he could change behind a velvet curtain just offstage.

Tim stood behind the curtain and removed his tennis shoes, socks, and jeans. This all seemed like an incredible dream to him. Someone tossed a green terry-cloth robe over the curtain for him to wear over his Speedo.

David looked at him admiringly once he came out from behind the curtain. "You are going to be fabulous," he reassured him.

Once the stylist had fixed his hair, he was asked to remove the robe and step into the shower. The lighting director needed to do some tests. He was asked to stand in various poses from different angles. He felt a bit awkward at first, moving about mechanically in front of a host of strangers, wearing nothing but a tiny pair of swimming trunks that barely contained his impressive package. There was a heated discussion between the director and the lighting expert about what was his best angle. It was decided he looked best filmed from his right side, which showed off his stunning profile and rippling abdominal muscles to greatest effect.

The makeup artist then touched up his face with a sponge smeared with a dark brown foundation. It felt greasy on his face.

"Don't worry. This is just a waterproof base to even out your complexion. It'll wash off with soap and water and a good washcloth." She bent down and began to apply the foundation to his stomach and chest, which tickled slightly and caused Tim to squirm a bit.

"Oh, ticklish are we?" the makeup artist teased. "It's a good thing you don't have a hairy chest. I can tell you are naturally smooth," she said with a flirtatious wink.

Next, she spritzed his entire body with a glossy, water-resistant spray to make his skin sparkle and glow under the lights. It would also help the water to bead on his skin, as on a freshly waxed car.

Finally, everything came together and the commercial was ready to be filmed. The director called for silence on the set. A buzzer sounded, and everyone stood in place. A stage assistant handed Tim a bar of lime-green soap. He stepped inside the shower set with the bar of soap in his hand. The mobile camera moved closer and zoomed in on his torso, which Tim could see on a closed-circuit TV screen just offstage. The showerhead was finally turned on, and Tim was asked to stand back from the stream of water so that his hair did not get wet. He had to move around the tub until the camera could film him from the waist up without the top of his Speedos in the shot. When he was at the perfect mark, filming began. He lathered his torso with the citrus-scented foam from the soap, flexing the muscles of his arms and chest. He smiled for the camera, the captivating smile that would soon melt the hearts of millions of people.

David felt a sense of pride as he saw how natural Tim looked on camera. The camera was going to love him, that much David knew from experience. Only a chosen few had the gift of being wholly natural and alluring at the same time, and Tim possessed that gift in spades.

The director yelled "Cut!" and the crew members clapped their hands. "That's a wrap," the director shouted.

Ruth and David came over to Tim as he stepped out of the shower. David handed him a towel and his robe. "You did great," he said, beaming with pride.

"Thanks. I owe all of this to you, you know."

"Oh, David here knows true talent when he sees it." Ruth lit up a cigarette and took a deep drag, allowing the smoke to fill her lungs before exhaling. "He's always had an eye for the fresh new face in town." She winked at Tim and reached out to pat him on his head, as if he were a little boy who had just done something to please his grandmother. "You'd better get yourself dressed now. No telling how many people around here will be wanting to jump your bones if you walk around in that tiny thing," she said, pointing to Tim's miniscule Speedo, "myself included!"

After Tim had washed away the makeup and changed his clothes, David and Ruth accompanied him to the studio commissary for a bite to eat. Tim kept his eyes peeled for stars as they went through the buffet line. Several daytime and prime-time television programs were taped at the studio, and the commissary was always a major hub of activity. He spotted an actor from his mother's favorite soap opera, *The Drifting Clouds,* at the front of the line, paying for a carton of yogurt and an apple.

The three selected their food and sat down to eat at a small table near the entrance to the commissary. Ruth regaled them with stories of her early days in New York and the golden age of Hollywood in the 1950s as Tim and David slowly ate their pastrami-on-rye sandwiches and sipped from their bottles of Perrier. Tim listened intently, enraptured as she told of her encounters with many old Hollywood legends, including a chance meeting with James Dean in the ladies' room of the Brown Derby restaurant in Hollywood, only weeks before his tragic death. Tim listened and laughed, and he could see why David had asked Ruth to be a part of his agency. She brought to the table a bit of the old-time glamour and fun that Hollywood used to represent.

As they were finishing their lunches, David noticed one of his newest clients had entered the commissary. He motioned the stunning blonde over to the table. Tim recognized her immediately. Her name was Raina Hawthorne, and she was on a sitcom that was currently one of the top-rated shows on television.

"Raina, my dear! How are things going over at *Ain't That a Shame?*" David asked as she approached the table.

Raina's violet eyes smiled at David. "It's fantastic. I'm having the time of my life, and I owe it all to you, of course."

"Don't I feel special? That's the second time someone has told me that today," David joked.

David introduced Raina to Tim, who was a bit starstruck and couldn't keep from staring at her. She was around the same age as Tim and had been a child star in commercials and television series. Her parents had immigrated to the States from her native New Zealand when she was six, knowing that their daughter had the makings of a star. She had seemingly avoided the sad fate of many of her contemporaries, former child stars who ended up destitute, drug addicted, insane, in prison, or dead. *Ain't That a Shame?* had debuted the previous season and was an immediate hit. She played the beautiful-but-brain-dead character of Katie, who wore lots of revealing outfits that showcased her shapely legs and ample bustline. Raina was now on the covers of many of the teen magazines and had her own best-selling poster that was hanging on the bedroom walls of hundreds of thousands of pubescent boys across the country.

"Tim is going to be a big star, mark my words," Ruth said with a smile. "What is your last name again, sweetheart?" Ruth asked.

"Gividend," he responded. "Like dividend with a 'G'."

"Oh, that will have to change, my dear. It doesn't have the right kind of oomph. Let's see, what can we change your name to? Tim Treasure? No, that's too feminine. Tim King, Tim Mortimer, Tim Maplewood. Help, you guys, I'm getting bupkis here."

"How about Tim Race?" Raina offered as she looked at Tim curiously, studying his features. "I think that has a nice ring to it, don't you?" she asked.

Tim looked at her and nodded his head. "I like the way that sounds."

Ruth clucked her tongue and examined Tim's face for herself. "Tim Race, huh? Gives the image of a masculine race-car driver. That does have a certain kind of appeal, wouldn't you say, David?"

David seemed to agree. "Yes, I like it. So, what do you think, Tim? Do you feel like changing your name?"

"If Ruth believes I should change my name, then that's exactly what I should do," he replied. He looked into Raina's violet eyes again. "Thank you for the suggestion, Raina."

"You're welcome, Tim Race." Raina gave Tim a friendly wink and treated him to yet another one of her beatific smiles.

A week later, it was mutually decided by David and Ruth that Tim had to move out of the motel and into more appropriate quarters. David offered the small guest cottage by the pool of his Malibu house, which Tim gratefully accepted. Of course, he would be spending most of his nights sharing David's bed, but he would at least have a bit of privacy with his own place.

He had taken the check he had received from the soap commercial and bought himself some new clothes. David had taken him shopping on Rodeo Drive one sparkling, early summer Saturday. Tim was impressed by all of the famous store names: Armani, Gucci, Christian Dior, Coco Chanel, Ralph Lauren, and Valentino. They drove to a small, chic boutique situated in an unimposing brownstone with an ivy-covered facade on the corner of Rodeo Drive and Wilshire Boulevard. The boutique was so exclusive there wasn't even a sign out front. The salesman was an old acquaintance of David's and happily took Tim's measurements for a new custom-made suit. The man spent an inordinate amount of time on his knees measuring Tim's inseam, and his hand came in contact with Tim's behind on more than one occasion. Tim took his rather obvious advances in stride. David made sure to tip the man well as they left the boutique and headed back to the Malibu Colony.

David had also enrolled him in some acting classes. If he was going to be an actor, then he was going to have to take some courses to hone his craft. He enjoyed attending class and progressed with ease. The instructor, a lovely woman in her early fifties with smooth, porcelain skin, told him he possessed an inner talent that came through whenever he was in character. It was the most wonderful compliment anyone had ever paid him.

When the April Showers commercial debuted during one of prime time's most-watched comedies, David invited Ruth and Raina over so they could all watch it together. They sat around, drinking martinis that Ruth made and eating microwave popcorn. When the commercial finally appeared, Tim felt a sudden rush of adrenaline at seeing himself on television. He thought about the millions of people across the country that were seeing his face and body at the same moment, and the skin on his arms became covered in goose bumps. Thirty seconds later, the commercial ended and David toasted Tim's success. Secretly, he wondered if his parents had seen the commercial back in Tenpole or if they even cared.

David and Tim made love that night, as they did most nights. The sex between them was magnificent, and he was a willing pupil for David to mold. Tim knew that he was falling for David's charms. He had been attracted to David immediately, of course. Tim knew that David was going to be instrumental in furthering his career, but that was not the only attraction. He truly cared for David, and he was certain the feeling was mutual.

A week after the commercial began to air nationally, David's agency received a call. It was from a casting director at the studio. They were casting for a new role in the long-running soap opera *The Drifting Clouds*. The character was a young, handsome drifter who arrives in the fictitious town of Whispering Springs, Montana, and has a secret past that links him to the soap's main family. The producer had seen Tim's commercial and thought that he had the look they were searching for to fill the role.

Tim was ecstatic when David told him the news. "Now, don't get your hopes up too high," he warned. "There is going to be a cattle call. There will probably be a few hundred other actors reading for the part, many who've had years more experience in the business than you've had."

Tim was not deterred. "I'm going to ace this audition," he said confidently.

"The producer you will be reading for is a big queen," David advised. "Play up to him. Flirt with him. Let him believe he has a chance to get into your pants. If you do, he'll be eating out of the palm of your hand."

Charles Norbit was one of the most successful producers of daytime dramas in the world. He had created many of the most popular soaps on television, including the top-rated *The Drifting Clouds,* which had debuted in 1970 and had remained the most-watched daytime drama on American television for more than a decade. He was indeed a legend in the industry, a well-respected producer with an astonishing twenty-five Emmy Awards to his credit. He had an eye for great storytelling and was responsible for some of the most provocative and moving storylines on daytime television. There were always buttons to push, Charles knew, always a new spin to put on an old and familiar story. He was famous for scouting out new talent, and the roster of re-nowned stars that had begun their careers on a Norbit drama was a veritable who's who of Hollywood royalty. He was equally famous, at least within the industry, for his penchant of seducing handsome young actors who were fresh arrivals in LA.

Tim made sure to leave early for his appointment, as David had in-formed him that Mr. Norbit was a stickler for punctuality. He was wearing the crisp new linen suit that had been custom-made for him. David had lent him the Mustang, and he maneuvered the car carefully through the bustle of the snarled LA traffic. He arrived at the immac-ulately appointed offices of Charles Norbit on Sunset Boulevard fif-teen minutes before his scheduled appointment. The pretty brunette secretary with the pleasant voice told him to have a seat and she would let him know when Mr. Norbit was ready to see him.

Ten minutes later, the secretary informed Tim that he could enter Mr. Norbit's office, and she led the way down a marble-floored corri-dor to a set of ornate double doors with brass doorknobs. She rapped lightly on the door and then proceeded to open it.

Charles Norbit was sitting at his enormous desk, smoking a contra-band Cuban cigar and typing furiously on his computer keyboard. The room was filled with the pungent and spicy odor of cigar smoke.

Charles continued to type, his glasses perched low on his nose as he stared intently at the computer screen.

"Excuse me, Mr. Norbit. Tim Race is here to read for the role of Jayson," the secretary chimed.

Charles looked up at Tim and the secretary and extinguished his cigar into a Lalique crystal ashtray. His expression softened as he removed his glasses and placed them on the desk. "Thank you, Tawny. That will be all. Hold the rest of my calls and make sure we are not disturbed."

The secretary nodded her head and smiled warmly at Tim as she left the room. Charles motioned for Tim to sit down in the chair directly across from him. Several of the Emmy Awards he had won over the years were on display in a glass case next to his desk. The window behind him framed a marvelous view of Hollywood and the surrounding area, the landmark Tower Records store just down the street.

"How are you today, Mr. Race?" Charles inquired as he reached across the desk to shake Tim's hand firmly. His voice was soft and friendly. "I hope I didn't keep you waiting very long."

"Not at all, sir. I am quite honored to even be asked to have a reading with you," he replied, showing off his most seductive smile. David had coached Tim on just the right things to say to him.

Charles lifted an age-spot-speckled hand to his forehead and scratched his brow lightly. His deep tan set off his watery blue eyes and the thick silver hair that covered the entire top of his head. His face showed his age of sixty-four, but it was still a very striking face, and the outline of how handsome he had been when he was younger could still be seen.

"As you know, I'm casting a new character for my soap *The Drifting Clouds*. The character is a young, rebellious drifter with a secret agenda who arrives in town to cause trouble for many of the established characters. He has to be sexy yet vulnerable. He has to exude a devil-may-care attitude that belies the fact that he has been horribly hurt and betrayed by his own family. The character will have many layers of emotional depth and resonance that will be uncovered as the plot plays itself out. Does this sound like something that would be of interest to you?" he asked, watching Tim's face closely from across the desk.

"Indeed, it sounds like a wonderful acting opportunity," was Tim's perfect response.

"I see that you don't actually have any acting experience, at least none on film. I've seen the video from your April Showers soap commercial, and you do possess a natural charm that the camera loves. Are you taking any acting lessons?"

Tim nodded his head. "Yes. I'm studying with Jane Lawrence."

"Jane's very good. In fact, many of the actors on my shows have studied under her. I would suggest you continue attending her classes." He paused for a moment. "How old are you?"

"I'm nineteen, sir." He prayed that wasn't too young for the role. "Almost twenty," he added quickly.

"That's perfect. Just the age I was envisioning for the character." He stood up from his chair and walked around the expansive desk until he was standing beside Tim. He handed him a piece of paper. "I'd like to read some lines with you, to see how well you do," he said as he pulled up a chair to face Tim. He sat very close to him and their knees touched slightly. Tim felt the warmth of Charles's knee pressing against his and swallowed back a touch of nervousness as he looked at the paper in his hand. He could smell the musk of his cologne mingled with the lingering scent of cigar smoke.

"Shall we take it from the top? You are reading for the character of Jayson, naturally. I'll set up the scene for you a bit so you'll know what direction to take. Jayson has just arrived in Whispering Springs, Montana, to seek out his natural mother, who gave him up for adoption when he was a baby. I'll read for the character of Skye, who is Jayson's young love interest."

The two read through the scene together. The scene required the character of Jayson to be angry and hostile toward his potential love interest. Tim stood up during one point in the script and thrashed his arms angrily in the air for effect.

When they had finished the scene, Charles got up from the chair. "That was very impressive, Tim. I think you captured Jayson's anger and frustration perfectly. I'd like for you to come in at a later date so we can videotape you doing a scene with the actress who plays Skye, Siobahn McCavandish. It's really just a formality, as I believe I've made my decision already. I think you would be excellent in this role. Would you like a drink to toast your latest success?"

Tim was beside himself but maintained his composure as to not give his true excitement away. "That would be lovely, Mr. Norbit," he responded with a smile.

"Please, call me Charlie, like everyone else around here does. What would you like, a gin and tonic? Bourbon? Rum and Coke?"

"Rum and Coke sounds good."

"I suppose I shouldn't be plying you with liquor as you are not yet of legal age, but I felt this was cause for a celebration. It's not every day that a newcomer to the acting profession gets cast in a plum role on a television soap opera," he commented as he mixed Tim's rum and Coke and poured himself an inch of an expensive cognac into a glass. He handed Tim his drink. "I hope you are appreciative of this opportunity that I'm giving to you," he added as his eyes surveyed the full length of Tim's body.

"Oh, I will be very appreciative, Mr. Norbit . . . I'm sorry, Charlie," he replied, flashing his mesmerizing smile at the older man. They were now speaking that unspoken language between men of a certain persuasion.

"Have a seat," Charles said, his mouth dry as he took a sip of his cognac.

Tim sat down on the chair and began to remove his jacket. Charles stared at him quietly before reaching his hand down to touch the waistband of Tim's slacks. Tim lifted his buttocks slightly from the chair and pressed his body harder against Charles's hand. Charles then reached up with both of his hands and began to unbutton Tim's shirt while Tim unbuckled his belt and pulled his pants down around his ankles. Tim sighed slightly as Charles moved upward across his chest and took a nipple into his mouth, first his right nipple and then the left. He lavished attention on the dark red nubs that quickly became erect from the stimulation of his mouth, teeth, and tongue. His tongue trailed lower, across the flat plain of his stomach, where it darted into the hidden fold of his navel. Tim ran his fingers across the thick hair on the older man's head, stroking the back of his neck and gently forcing his face downward. Charles was only too eager to claim the hardening prize that awaited him beneath the silk fabric of Tim's boxers.

Twenty minutes later they were finished with their business and were straightening up their clothing. Charles noticed a small, wet stain on the crotch of Tim's new pants. "I can give you the name of a wonderful dry cleaner in Hollywood to get the stain out of that nice suit of yours," he told Tim. "They are discreet and never ask any questions."

Tim shook his head as he removed a tissue from a dispenser on the desk and blotted lightly at the stain. "That's okay. I'll have it taken care of. Is there anything I need to sign? A contract or something for the role on *The Drifting Clouds?*"

"I'll be in contact with your agent. We'll hash out all the small details." He walked over to Tim and extended his hand. "Nice meeting you, Tim Race, and I'm looking forward to working with you."

David asked how the meeting had gone when he arrived back at the Malibu house later that afternoon. Tim told him to expect a call from Charles Norbit any day. David was so pleased and proud.

"So, did you take my advice and play up to him like I told you?" he asked.

Tim smiled tightly. "Just a little."

"Skye, you know how I feel about you. You've known from the moment I arrived in town. Why are you pretending you don't care about me?"

"Because I *don't* care about you! In fact, I don't care if you drop off the face of the earth, Jayson Weldon!" The camera zoomed in for a close-up of the stunning redhead's face and held it for a few seconds.

"Cut!" the director yelled. The lights went back on in the studio, and the cast and crew of *The Drifting Clouds* scurried onto the next set location.

Tim approached his beautiful costar, Siobahn McCavandish. Tim had been with the show for more than nine months and the two had formed a friendly relationship. Tim was well liked on the set. Most people were drawn to his handsome looks and gregarious personality.

"Great work today, as always, Siobahn," Tim told her with sincerity as they both headed toward their dressing rooms. Siobahn was a very talented actress and had received an Emmy Award for Outstanding Younger Actress for her exceptional work on the show the year before.

"Thank you, darling. Every scene with you always brings out the best in me," she replied in her natural Georgia drawl, which she successfully concealed on the show. "The next scene should be a challenge, though. I have to smack you hard right across the face!"

Tim laughed. "Maybe I'll play another practical joke on you; then it won't be so hard for you to be angry enough to slap me," he teased. Siobahn's easygoing nature made her the target of many of the practical jokers on the set, Tim being one of the worst. He was a twenty-year-old man but still retained the spirit of a young boy.

"That won't be necessary, I assure you," Siobahn replied with a smile on her face.

Later that day, Tim had a meeting with Charles Norbit. Mr. Norbit was a hands-on producer and had monthly meetings with every actor who starred in one of his dramas. He enjoyed chatting with the stars who helped make his shows so popular, and he liked getting feedback from each actor. Charles wanted to let Tim know that he felt he was doing a fantastic job in his role of Jayson and that he was quite pleased with his own intuition in selecting Tim for the job. Tim allowed Charles to express his appreciation by pulling down Tim's tight-fitting denims and treating him to yet another expert blow job.

Just before Tim was to set to leave the studio after a busy twelve-hour day of filming, Siobahn ran over to him and pulled him into a huge embrace.

"They just announced the Emmy nominations! You and I have both been selected in the Outstanding Younger Actor and Actress categories!"

Tim was literally nonplussed. They actually considered him worthy of an Emmy Award?

"I can't believe it," he sputtered, searching Siobahn's face to see whether she was playing a trick to get back at him for all the pranks he had pulled on her over the past nine months. "Are you teasing me?"

Just then, several other actors from the show as well as a few of the camera people came over to offer both Siobahn and Tim congratulations on their nominations.

Within minutes, Tim had exited the studio and was on his way to the house in Malibu, eager to share the fantastic news with David. He pulled the Mustang into the driveway and bounded into the house. Inside, he noticed that the living room and dining area were lit with the soft glow of candlelight. A bottle of champagne was chilling in a pail of ice, and Emilia, David's maid, was bringing out a covered dish on a platinum serving tray. She had worked for David's family since the early 1980s, practically from the day she had arrived in the United States, seeking asylum from her war-ravaged native country of El Salvador. When David had left home to live in Los Angeles, he brought Emilia along with him, much to the chagrin of his parents.

"Good evening, Mr. Race," she said in her thick accent, her long, straight black hair pulled into a bun that rested on top of her head. "Mr. Reardon say he will be down shortly for dinner."

Tim smiled at Emilia. He had been trying to win her over since he had moved into David's home, but Emilia had yet to warm to him. Tim thought that perhaps she didn't approve of his relationship with her employer, feeling that he was too young and green for someone older and more respectable like David. David just laughed it off, of course, but it still bothered Tim, who was used to everyone liking him.

"*Gracias,* Emilia," he replied in his most convincing accent, secretly wishing that he had paid more attention to his lessons in high school Spanish.

Emilia waddled her short, squat frame back into the kitchen while Tim surveyed the sumptuous contents on the dining-room table. Of course David was already aware of his Emmy nomination; David was a Hollywood insider, after all. He had connections in all the right places, one of the many things Tim loved about him.

"I hear that congratulations are in order." It was David's voice, coming from the living room. He carried a large bouquet of deep crimson roses, carefully wrapped in red cellophane and delicate tissue paper embossed with the symbol of Fred Hayman's Emporium on Rodeo Drive. "These are for you," he said softly as he handed Tim the bouquet.

Tim smiled broadly and tears formed in his eyes. No one had ever taken the time to buy him flowers before; it was such a simple yet romantic gesture.

"Thank you, baby. This is so sweet of you," Tim said as he bent down to take in the intoxicating aroma of the fresh roses.

"You've earned it and so much more," David said with an air of mystery, kissing Tim on the crown of his head. "I'm incredibly proud of you."

They kissed each other tenderly, and then David took the roses away to place into a lovely heirloom Tiffany decanter that had been a gift from his deceased grandmother upon his graduation, magna cum laude, from Stanford University.

"Now, don't they look beautiful?" he asked. "Well, I'm absolutely famished. It looks like Emilia has prepared a magnificent celebratory repast, so let's eat."

After the two had dined on the marvelous meal and toasted Tim's Emmy nomination with the bottle of champagne, David informed him that he would be visiting his parents in San Francisco over the weekend. He asked Tim if he wanted to go along, unsure how he would react. Tim readily said yes to the invitation, as he was curious about David's family. David so very rarely spoke of them, but he knew that they were a wealthy, well-connected family from old money.

"Do they know about your . . . lifestyle?" Tim asked.

"Yes, they do. I mean, I never actually came out and told my mother or father that I'm gay, but they'd have to be blind or ignorant not to realize. I am a thirty-three-year-old confirmed bachelor living in LA, after all," he said with a laugh.

Tim acknowledged the fact that David was a little sensitive about his age, so he never brought up the topic around him. Tim knew that David was actually thirty-four, soon to be thirty-five; he had sneaked a peek at his driver's license one day while David was in the shower. He was also careful not to mention the medicine cabinet full of antiwrinkle creams and potions in the bathroom. Age was certainly not an issue to Tim, who was attracted to men of varying ages, but he did not wish to make David overly sensitive to the fact that he was more than a decade older than his fresh-faced paramour.

That weekend, David and Tim drove up the scenic California coastline to San Francisco in Tim's slightly used Mercedes. He was earning more than $1,200 an episode on *The Drifting Clouds,* and David was only too happy to cosign the loan for him.

They took their time reaching San Francisco, stopping at places of interest along the way and taking photographs. Once they arrived, they hopped on one of the famed cable cars and explored the sites of the city for a while. Its incredible beauty and vitality astounded Tim. The duo made a quick pilgrimage to both Castro Street and Haight-

Ashbury, where the gay and bohemian subcultures were still very much alive and thriving.

By the time they pulled up to the rambling, thirty-room Beaux-Arts mansion on prestigious Nob Hill, where David had spent his youth, the sun was beginning to wane. David informed him that the exterior of the home had taken a beating from the massive earthquake a few years earlier. The east wing of the house, which was still under-going repairs, had scaffolding on the outside and was draped in a green tarpaulin. There was an unparalleled view of the city from the house, however, and the bay and bridge could be seen on those days when the fog lifted.

An immaculately dressed butler greeted the two at the front door. "Good to see you home again, Mr. Reardon," the older gentleman said with a smile reflecting genuine warmth.

"It's good to see you again as well, Franklin. I hope my parents have been treating you well," David said.

"Oh, Mr. and Mrs. Reardon have always treated with me with great respect and kindness, which is why I have remained in their em-ploy for almost thirty years."

David led the way down the foyer with the marble floors to the house's impressive great room. Expensive, antique Victorian furniture abounded, and an eclectic artwork collection covered the walls. A cherished Matisse, a perpetual conversation piece, hung over the fire-place. David's mother, Alicia, was an avid art collector. She usually made several trips a year to Europe and New York to attend auctions at Sotheby's or Christie's or at smaller, lesser-known galleries, where she could spot a priceless work of art from fifty yards away.

David's father, Samuel Adams Reardon III, was drinking brandy from a snifter and reading the *Wall Street Journal* in the library, which housed a collection of over thousands of books, many of them rare first editions. He was a handsome man and looked very much like David, although with graying hair and a few wrinkles that gave him the look of a highly distinguished gentleman. He was very cordial to Tim, as he queried David on his life in Los Angeles and the economic status of his agency.

After making chitchat for a half hour, David excused the two of them, saying they were tired and wanted to rest and wash up before dinner. They climbed the ornate staircase to the second floor of the mammoth house. David showed Tim the bedroom where he had slept as a boy. The room had not been altered in any way since David had moved out to attend Stanford many years before.

"This is the bed where I lost my virginity," he said matter-of-factly, pointing to the enormous four-poster Queen Anne with the billowing canopy. "I was attending private school and brought home a schoolmate of mine, Matthew. We were both sixteen, and I guess he was experimenting with his sexuality. We did each other sixty-nine style and shot our wads on the neatly pressed Laura Ashley sheets that my mother purchased from Marks and Spencer in London. Heaven knows what the maid thought about the stains. I believe Matthew is a politician with a homophobic agenda and living in Boston now, married with three kids."

"Sounds far more glamorous than my first time," Tim countered, thinking back to the lonely bus station on the New Mexico border and the older stranger. That seemed like a lifetime ago. So much had changed since then, and he felt like a different person altogether.

"If it makes you feel any better, I also brought back to my room a tattooed, leather-clad hustler I picked up on the Embarcadero," David teased. "It was during the stage when I was rebelling against the Establishment."

After David had showed Tim practically every room in the house, a bell chimed precisely three times, announcing that dinner was being served. They went downstairs to find Alicia already at the mahogany dining room table that seated twenty-five. She was a woman of great beauty and exquisite taste, and she was old-money thin, which meant she was borderline anorexic. Her chestnut-colored hair was perfectly coiffed and her face had been pulled tight during a recent trip to Brazil, where she had gone to seek out the talents of a world-renowned plastic surgeon. The surgeon owned his own private island off the coast of Rio de Janeiro and had reportedly lifted the well-known faces of such luminaries as Jacqueline Kennedy Onassis and Sophia Loren.

Samuel soon joined them for dinner, and a host of servants brought out course after course of delicious food. Samuel queried about Tim's occupation, and David patiently explained that he was a client with his agency. David's father complained vociferously to his only child, for the hundredth time, that he was disappointed his son had not wanted to be a part of the family business. David, Samuel was proud to tell, was the scion of the original Samuel Adams Reardon, who had founded a steel and shipping empire that had earned the family more money than could be spent by fifty generations of spendthrift Reardons.

Mrs. Reardon seemed interested in Tim's acting career and asked question after question, even though she very rarely watched television. Tim was polite in answering her questions, although he could tell that she hadn't the faintest inkling what he was talking about.

Once the dessert of crème brûlée had been served, David was ready to end the familial version of the Spanish Inquisition. He excused the two of them from the table, even though Tim had not finished his dessert.

When they were alone in the great room, David let out a sigh and wiped his brow. "I didn't think that was ever going to end. Positively excruciating. I'm sorry to have to put you through all of that. My parents can be a bit much," he said wearily.

"I thought things went pretty well, actually. I found both of your parents to be quite nice."

"You are too kind, my love. I thought that perhaps they would take the hint that you and I are lovers, but I believe they have a mental block when it comes to my homosexuality," David said, rolling his eyes.

David and Tim remained in the great room and talked for several hours. David appeared to be in a confessional mood at his parents' home, and he entertained Tim with stories of his college exploits, detailing his sexual peccadilloes over the years. Tim thought that it had been a good idea to join David on his trip back to the family homestead. It gave him insight into why David was the way that he was.

After midnight, when David's parents had already retired to their separate bedrooms and the servants had settled into their private quarters, the two tiptoed upstairs.

Like a scene from an old-fashioned, romantic movie, they stood outside the door of the guest room, where Tim would be spending the night alone.

"I guess I should actually be respectful of my family for a change. No more rebellion or teenage experimentation to muddle my way through. You'll be all right sleeping alone in the guest room tonight, won't you?" David asked, as he gently stroked the back of Tim's neck.

"I think I'll survive. Let's just not make a habit of spending nights apart."

In the faint light of the corridor, David's face looked as young and innocent as a schoolboy's. "I love you more than anything," he whispered softly into Tim's ear.

Tim fell into David's warm, accepting embrace. "I love you, too."

"Goodnight, sweetheart," David murmured softly and turned away to walk down the corridor to his own bedroom, to sleep in the bed where he grew up, dreaming of life and love and all of the wonderful things that children expect the world to present to them on a silver platter.

Tim waited until he saw the door to David's room close, then entered his room, the thought of how fortunate he was filling him with a wonderful kind of happiness.

★ 5

"For lives that are always changing . . . like The Drifting Clouds."

The familiar words, now part of the popular culture, emanated from the television in Ruth's spacious Century City office. They were immediately followed by the melodic theme music and the chyron featuring the name of the show positioned over a bank of fluffy white clouds set in a cerulean blue sky. The opening theme music and image had been changed and updated several times over the past twenty-odd years, but the introductory statement, timeless and perfect, had remained the same.

It was mid-September, and the Reardon & Borstein Talent Agency was abuzz with activity. Ruth was on the telephone, reconfirming airline reservations to New York to attend the Emmy Awards ceremony in a few days' time.

"These airline people are such *schmucks,*" Ruth said to Tim, who was seated across from her cluttered desk thumbing through a year-old copy of *Esquire* magazine. "If they've messed up our plans—Yes, I'm still here."

Tim chuckled softly and shook his head, putting the magazine down. The commercial had ended and the show had returned to the small screen mounted on the wall above Ruth's head. It was a love scene between Skye and Jayson, who had finally consummated their tempestuous relationship by literally rolling in the hay of a horse barn. Tim was shirtless in the scene and, as he watched himself on television, he had to admit he was indeed damn sexy.

The viewing audience apparently agreed with that sentiment. Thousands of letters from breathless female fans arrived at the studio on a weekly basis, proclaiming their undying love for Jayson Weldon. Jayson and Skye were now officially what the soap world dubbed a *super couple.* Tim and Siobahn McCavandish were being interviewed together practically every week, and the winsome duo had appeared on the cover of *Soap Opera Digest*—the industry bible—several times in the past year.

Tim, David, Ruth, and Raina would be flying to New York together. Raina was going as Tim's "date." When asked about his romantic life in interviews, Tim was usually vague, saying that he was "too busy" with his career to be seriously dating anyone. David was the one who had suggested that Raina attend the Emmy Awards as Tim's date. Raina had accepted the offer joyously. She had been dating an older man, a writer for *Ain't That a Shame?* But the relationship had recently ended, and Raina had no interest in pursuing a new one, so, for the time being, she was willing to be Tim's beard.

"Well, it looks like all of our travel arrangements are finally in order," Ruth said with a look of relief on her face. She'd been on the telephone with the airline for over a half hour. "I've made reservations for the four of us to stay at the Waldorf-Astoria. It was a bitch to make the reservations so late, but fortunately they could accommodate us. It will be fun to hit the old neighborhood in Queens and see my boatload of relatives again."

"I can't wait to see New York. I've never been, you know," Tim said with excitement in his voice.

"A boy like you can get into a lot of trouble in New York," Ruth cautioned as she lit up an unfiltered cigarette. "David and I will have to be your chaperones."

"You guys won't be able to watch me every second," Tim joked, just as the closing credits for *The Drifting Clouds* began to scroll down the television screen.

Early on a Thursday morning, the group of four boarded a flight from LAX bound for New York. Tim and Raina sat together in first class with David and Ruth seated across the aisle from them. Tim was a bit anxious; this was his first time aboard an airplane.

"What are you going to do if you win the award?" Raina asked Tim after the flight attendant had served them their Cokes and tiny bags of chocolate chip cookies.

"God, I don't know. It makes me sweat just thinking about it. Anyway, I probably don't have anything to worry about. I won't win. There's some stiff competition in my category."

"I don't know, Tim. You have as good a chance at winning as anyone else," Raina said, taking a nibble from a cookie.

The remainder of the flight was smooth and uneventful. Upon their arrival at LaGuardia, they were greeted by a uniformed chauffeur holding a cardboard placard with David's name written on it. After they picked up their luggage, the driver escorted them to a waiting limousine to whisk them into Manhattan in grand style. Tim thrilled at the sight of the magnetic New York skyline as they crossed the East River via the Queensboro Bridge; Raina immediately began telling Tim about each landmark they encountered. From there, it was a quick trip to the majestic Waldorf-Astoria on Park Avenue and East Fiftieth Street. Tim had butterflies in his stomach as the limousine came to a stop in front of the Art Deco towers that constituted the hotel, which encompassed an entire city block.

"The duke and duchess of Windsor lived here at one time," Raina commented as they entered the plush lobby where presidents and royalty, movie stars and billionaires had all once stood. They passed the gigantic clock in the central lobby, created for the 1893 World's Fair, on their way to check into the hotel. Ruth pointed out the bas-relief friezes and elegant iron grillwork, which perfectly set off the beautifully painted murals, dark mahogany paneling, and stately columns.

After checking in, David and Ruth told Tim and Raina to go on up to their rooms while they stayed behind to take care of some business. The harried but smiling porter transported their luggage up to their adjoining suites as Tim and Raina rushed toward the elevator.

Once in his room, Tim began to check out all of the suite's accoutrements. He hopped onto the bed to check its softness before inspecting the contents of the room's fully stocked minibar, replete with exorbitantly priced goodies. A remote control device opened and closed the expensive yet understated draperies that, when opened, revealed a stunning view of Upper Midtown. From the window, Tim could see the white-marbled, twin spires of St. Patrick's Cathedral on Fifth Avenue, which stood in stark contrast to the onyx black facade of the Olympic Tower, situated directly across from the Gothic Revival church. To the south, the gleaming turrets of the Chrysler Building and the Empire State Building stood solemn sentinel over the city.

"Stop playing with that," Raina admonished, after Tim had opened and closed the drapes six or seven times. "You would think that you grew up in a cave."

"Well, I'm sorry I didn't grow up with a silver spoon in my mouth like someone I know," Tim retorted good-naturedly. "All of this," he said, gesturing around the room, "still fascinates me. Besides, I did grow up in a cave."

"You'd better get used to all the glitz and glamour, my friend. You are, after all, a bona fide star now."

The telephone rang. Tim picked up the line.

"Tim, you and Raina can meet me at the Peacock Alley lounge downstairs in the lobby. We've got to go and pick up our tuxedos before the shop closes at seven."

"We'll be right down," Tim said, replacing the phone carefully on the receiver.

"I believe that piano once belonged to Cole Porter," Raina said as they entered the illustrious Peacock Alley cocktail lounge.

"You really should get a job working for Circle Line tours, Raina." David was waiting at the bar, a gin and tonic in his hand.

Raina pulled a face and stuck out her tongue at David. "I'm knowledgeable about New York. So sue me. Where's Ruth?"

"She's taking the subway out to Queens to visit her sisters. We may never see her again," David said with a laugh.

From a darkened corner of the lounge, a middle-aged woman wearing a green leisure suit approached Tim.

"Oh, my heaven," she trilled in a pronounced New England accent that Tim couldn't quite place. "You're Jayson Weldon from *The Drifting Clouds*! I just simply love you and Skye together on the show! All of my friends back in New Hampshire will just die when they hear that I've met you. May I please have your autograph?"

Even though it was beginning to occur more frequently, it still caught Tim off guard whenever fans recognized him while in public.

Tim blushed slightly. "Of course," he said, flashing his million-dollar smile. "Would you like Raina Hawthorne's autograph as well?" he asked as the woman handed him a cocktail napkin to sign.

"Who's Raina Hawthorne?" the woman inquired.

Raina grimaced and shot Tim a withering look. "No one important, I'm sure," she said, as Tim suppressed the desire to laugh.

Once she had taken an entire roll of film with her camera, the ecstatic fan said her good-byes and went to seek out the gaggle of women that had accompanied her on a theater and museum excursion to New York.

"The many perks of being a star," David said playfully to both Tim and Raina. "It's getting late, so we'd better get to the tuxedo rental place."

When they exited the hotel and stepped out onto Park Avenue, the sun had already begun to set and the city was awash in a brilliant, golden light. Tim could feel the pulse of the city beating mightily from beneath the concrete pavement. They made their way toward Fifth Avenue two blocks down, turning right on the celebrated street. Along the way, they passed Rockefeller Center and Radio City Music Hall, where the Daytime Emmy Awards ceremony was to be broadcast live the following evening. David took lead of the pack, taking long, purposeful strides in a rush to make it to Trump Tower, eight blocks away. Traffic was heavy along the thoroughfare; hundreds of yellow taxis were ushering their important occupants to their imposing apartments on the Upper East Side.

The night was beginning to turn cool, and Tim offered his light jacket to Raina, who had folded her arms across her chest for warmth. Finally, the trio arrived outside Trump Tower. Next door was the discreet treasure of Tiffany & Co., where Raina couldn't resist striking an Audrey Hepburn–like pose outside the luxurious window display of jewels fit for a queen. Tim marveled at the lavish six-story atrium of pink marble, waterfalls, and mirrors once they entered Trump Tower, which opened up to reveal layer after layer of exclusive boutiques and ultra-chic cafés.

"Why didn't you guys just bring your own tuxedos from Los Angeles?" Raina asked, puzzled as to why they would do all of this rushing around Manhattan. All tuxedos looked the same to her: boring and indistinguishable from one another. She had brought her own designer gown by Givenchy from LA, carefully wrapped in a garment bag and stored in an indestructible trunk.

"Because, my dear, if we had brought our own, they would have been all wrinkled from the flight and would have required dry cleaning, which we do not have the time for," David explained.

After they picked up their tuxedos and had them dispatched to the Waldorf by valet, David received a call on his mobile from Ruth. She wanted to meet up at the Temple Emanu-El off Fifth Avenue so they could all eat dinner together. Raina was able to hail a taxi fairly quickly after several minutes of failed attempts by both David and Tim. The taxi made slow progress up Fifth Avenue, the snarl of early evening traffic reaching its zenith at the intersection with Central Park South. They found Ruth waiting outside the bronze grille doors of the impressive limestone Temple Emanu-El, one of the largest synagogues in the world. Ruth was smoking a cigarette, which she quickly tossed to the pavement and extinguished with the well-worn heel of her leather, slingback pump.

"I just thought I should make amends for some of my sins over the years," Ruth said hoarsely as she squeezed into the crowded taxi, sitting partially on Tim's lap. "I also wanted to say hello to the spirit of my late husband, Edgar. We were married here in 1945, two days after he returned home from the European campaign in World War II. He was a good man, may he rest in peace until I get there," she said, looking upward.

"So, where are we going to eat?" Tim asked, his stomach in knots with hunger. He hadn't eaten anything since his meal on the airplane.

"How about Italian? There's Felidia's over on East Fifty-Eighth Street that serves a fabulous *gnocchi al ragu d'agrello* that's simply to die for," Ruth suggested.

"Sounds perfect," David responded, reaching over without thought and brushing lint from Tim's shoulder. The day had been a long one, and he just wanted to eat dinner and return to the hotel for some rest, as the next day was going to be incredibly hectic.

Tim, on the other hand, was still full of energy, the electrical current emitted by New York invigorating his body and spirit. He had already fallen for the overwhelming charisma of the city, and he was certain that he would be spending more time here in the future.

Later on that evening, after they had all gorged themselves on the wonderful Italian food and vintage wine at Felidia's, Tim and Raina decided that it was far too early to call it a night and wanted to explore the city for a while more. Both David and Ruth begged off, claiming exhaustion. They said their good-byes, but not before David advised Tim to make sure to call it an early night, for he had to look his most beautiful best at the awards show.

Tim and Raina decided to take a quick walk over to Central Park. They rented a hansom carriage with an English driver who took them through the park, passing by the Children's Zoo and the Wollman Rink and along the transverse road until they reached Central Park West. The leafy green ocean of the park was the only boundary between the Upper East and Upper West Sides, but they were worlds apart in many aspects. The sky above was cloudless, and there was a crescent moon watching over them. Tim and Raina huddled close to each other, pulling the muslin blanket provided by the carriage driver up to the bottoms of their chins.

The moment proved to be too romantic for Raina, who suddenly tilted her face upward to give Tim a kiss, neither passionate nor chaste, on his mouth.

He stared back at her, more than a little surprised. "Where did that come from?" he asked, watching her face, illuminated by the lights from the Upper West Side.

The only sounds were the steady *clippity-clop* of the horse's hooves hitting the asphalt and the gentle grinding of the carriage's wheels. "I simply couldn't pass up the opportunity," she explained quietly, nestling her head into the wide groove between his shoulder and neck.

"It wouldn't be right not to have a romantic kiss on a hansom carriage ride in Central Park on a remarkable September night such as this."

"I see your point," he said with a contented smile, kissing the curls on top of her head and pulling his arm tighter around her diminutive waist.

★ 6

"Tim, darling. Best of luck on winning tonight," intoned Janice Cooperman, the grande dame of *The Drifting Clouds,* her voice raspy from a two-pack-a-day smoking habit. She was touching the enormous yellow diamond necklace lavishly draped around the crepey skin of her neck, which no amount of face-lifts could erase. She had been with the show from day one and was the only remaining original cast member. Janice was idolized on the set and was known for taking newcomers under her wing and giving them guidance and advice, and she had always been kind and helpful to Tim.

"Thank you, Janice. Good luck to you as well," Tim said respectfully. Janice had been nominated twelve times over the years but had never won the coveted prize.

Radio City Music Hall was filled to capacity for the awards ceremony. Tim and Raina were seated together in the front row reserved for the nominees and their dates. Siobahn McCavandish was seated to Tim's right with her boyfriend, an out-of-work actor who had put the moves on Tim while they were in the bathroom together moments earlier. Tim had turned the guy down flat, even though he was quite good-looking in a fake-tan, California-plastic kind of way. David and Ruth were seated two rows behind them. David always made sure to arrange things so that he was just out of camera range whenever he attended a public event with Tim; he didn't want any damaging photographic evidence to pop up and cause tongues to wag.

When Raina and Tim had entered the auditorium on each other's arms, the photographers and reporters had gone wild. The two made an absolutely stunning couple and heads turned wherever they went. Raina's pale pink, full-length beaded gown with almost-invisible spaghetti straps set against her alabaster skin made her look like an exotic princess from a Scandinavian country. Tim thought back to the tender kiss that the two had shared the previous night in Central Park.

Their relationship had transcended mere friendship and had crossed over to something else.

Charles Norbit sauntered past Tim on the way to his seat, and he gave Tim a warm smile. "Good luck, son," he whispered into his ear, patting him on the shoulder.

As the ceremony commenced, Tim grew more and more nervous. The emcees chatted amiably, reading lame jokes, written by someone else, from the TelePrompTer, followed by polite laughter and applause. The first category to be announced was the Outstanding Younger Actress. As the list of nominees was being read, Tim mouthed a "you're going to win" to Siobahn, who smiled back nervously and crossed her fingers. Her date gave Tim a childish scowl.

When Siobahn's name was called, Tim and Raina jumped to their feet, followed quickly by the rest of the cast from the show. The thunderous applause was deafening as Siobahn rushed to the stage to accept her second Emmy Award in as many years. In her teary-eyed speech, she thanked Tim for being such a terrific costar to work with, for which Tim blew her a kiss, caught on live television.

There was a brief commercial break before the show returned to the airwaves. Tim tried to gather his composure, aware his category was up next. He turned around to see David, who gave him a reassuring wink. Raina squeezed his clammy hand firmly in both of hers.

Applause broke out as the show began again after the break. An actor and actress from a rival soap, who had won awards the previous year, were to announce the nominees in the category. Tim steeled himself, wishing that he had at least prepared an acceptance speech on the off chance that he won the award.

Tim, his heart pounding loudly in his ears, did not hear the names of the nominees being read. He was aware when the camera was on him as his name was announced, for he could see his face on the ubiquitous monitors hanging overhead.

"And the award goes to," the actress said, pausing dramatically before breaking the seal on the envelope containing the winner's name, "Seth Williams, from *Yesterday, Today, and Tomorrow!*"

There was more applause as the young actor, who had been with the soap since he was nine years old, bounded up to the podium to accept his much-deserved award.

"Well, those are the breaks," Tim said, only slightly disappointed.

"There's always next year, you know," Raina replied, still very proud of Tim's achievements.

"That's true. Who knows, maybe I'll be doing something even greater than working on a soap by this time next year."

During the next commercial interlude, David and Ruth came over to offer Tim encouragement and consolation, neither of which he needed, but it felt good to have them offer it regardless.

David chucked Tim lightly beneath the chin with his fist. "Believe me, just the nomination will do wonders for your career now. I've told you this before, but I believe that you are going places in showbiz."

"Do you really believe that?" Tim asked, wondering if his loss tonight had altered his opinion.

"Absolutely," David reassured, just as everyone was told by a booming voice over the loudspeaker to take his or her seat once again.

The show, like in that old Broadway cliché, must go on.

7

March 1993

From across Charles Norbit's massive desk, Tim repeatedly tapped the toe of his brand-new, very expensive leather sneaker against the leg of the chair in which he was seated. Charles was droning on in a staccato voice, but Tim no longer heard what he was saying. The only words that kept reverberating in his mind over and over again were "I'm afraid that we will be releasing you from your contract, Tim."

He was being fired. Tossed aside. Thrown away. Handed his walking papers. This could not be happening, he thought to himself. He had given everything he had for his role as Jayson Weldon. Fan mail continued to pour in from around the country. He had been nominated for a fucking Emmy Award, for Christ's sake!

"So, if there aren't any questions, if you will please sign this release form, Tawny will give you your final paycheck and you can be on your way. Once you've cleared out your dressing room, you may leave the key with the guard at the front gate of the studio." Charles spoke with the icy professionalism of a diplomat asking a world leader to sign a contract of disarmament.

Tim forced his mind to clear so that he could respond. "You're actually firing me? I don't understand," was all that he could muster.

"As I've already explained, we are taking Skye and Jayson's story line in a different direction. It's nothing personal, you understand. I simply have to do what I feel is best for the continued success of the show."

Nothing personal, Tim thought sarcastically. *What a total crock of shit.* Then, it dawned on him: Mr. Norbit had found a new, fresh-faced actor that he wanted to try out in the role of Jayson. He could picture him in his mind: an innocent neophyte, just off the bus from Kansas or South Dakota, who was only too willing to let Charles suck his corn-fed, gargantuan cock and hand him Tim's job without so much as a thought for his well-being or happiness. David had been right all along; showbiz was a heartless bitch goddess.

"I suppose I should thank you for the opportunity that you gave me," Tim said as he stood up from the chair. "I must confess, you do give one hell of a blow job," he added condescendingly.

Charles shook his head in disgust. "Now, let's not make things unpleasant, Tim. We both got what we wanted out of this relationship. I am sure that you will go on to greater things."

"That, Mr. Norbit, you can bet money on," Tim said with supreme confidence before he signed the release forms and tossed the pen carelessly onto Charles's desk.

He left the office and stormed down the corridor. Tawny had a sorrowful look on her face as he approached her office cubicle.

"I'm so sorry about the way things turned out, Mr. Race," she said in her still-pleasant voice, her eyes brimming with tears as she handed him his last paycheck. "Best of luck to you in the future."

"Thank you, Tawny. That means a great deal."

He marched over to the bank of elevators, paycheck in hand. He had to see David. He would have thought that David would have had some sort of inside information, a clue to warn him in advance of his impending unemployment. Then he realized that there was nothing in his contract that stated there would be a written press release when he was going to be fired. There was no such thing as job security in the entertainment industry, he was now beginning to realize.

Tim fumbled in his pants pocket for the keys to the Mercedes once he reached the parking lot. It was a rare, cloudy day in Los Angeles, and the hot, dry Santa Ana winds were blowing fiercely from the northeast, dust and debris swirling into a mini-vortex across the pavement. Low, churning clouds scudded ominously across the sky. He jumped into the car and pressed his foot hard against the accelerator, in a rush to make it to David's office in Century City.

"I don't believe it," David shouted. "They couldn't possibly have fired you!"

"Well, believe it. I just came from the bigwig's office and he told me directly to my face."

Ruth had entered the room once she heard the commotion. "What's going on?" she queried, a worried look on her face.

"I've been fired, that's what," Tim bellowed harshly, before realizing it was Ruth with whom he was speaking. His voice softened. "As you can tell, I'm more than a little upset."

"Of course you are, my darling," Ruth consoled in a soothing, motherly tone of voice. "Being fired in this town is always such an ugly thing. Nothing private and everyone knowing your business. But it happens to the best of them. I couldn't name a single actor who hasn't been fired at least once, so you are certainly in some esteemed company."

David concurred. "Ruth is right, of course. This business is absolutely brutal, something I have warned you about from the start. Think of this as just a temporary setback, a pause before the beginning of bigger and brighter things for you."

Tim managed a weak smile. "I know that you guys are right, but it still feels like I've been run over by a steamroller."

"You'll grow accustomed to that feeling eventually," Ruth said without the slightest hint of irony.

"This could be it. This could be just what we've been hoping for," David said by telephone, long distance from London. "There's a director over here who's trying to find the next Bruce Lee, only he wants an all-American type. He's planning on doing a series of low-budget action-adventure movies, kind of like Rambo, only leaner and better-looking."

Tim found the idea intriguing, especially in light of his six-month-long, forced sabbatical. "Me, an action-adventure hero? Sounds pretty awesome, but do you think the director will go for it?"

"It's all in the sack," David replied, immediately regretting his choice of words. He then raised his voice a slight octave. "I mean in the bag."

Tim didn't really want to know what else David was doing in London besides conducting business from his suite in the Savoy. They had adopted a "don't ask, don't tell" policy when it came to their love life, which suited Tim just fine. Still, he had to admit, he felt a tiny pang of jealously at the thought of David with someone else. Not that Tim was a Catholic-school choirboy by any stretch of the imagination.

"I'm heading home tonight, my love. I'll arrange things with the director. In a few weeks' time, you will be flying off to exotic Southeast Asia to shoot your first theatrical release."

"From your mouth to God's ear," Tim said, praying that this deal went through. It was hard going without his own money once he had become accustomed to earning it, even though David was kind enough to lend him whatever he needed to pay for things. It didn't feel right to Tim, though; he had his pride and wanted to earn his own keep.

"Nothing to worry about. I promised you that I was going to get your career back on the right trajectory, did I not?"

"Yes, you did. Now hurry back home. I miss holding you next to me in bed at night."

"I'm touching you now. Can't you feel my hand on your dick?" David breathed sexily into the phone.

Tim felt his dick stiffen beneath the constraints of his exercise shorts. He had been working out a great deal lately, mostly to let off the tension of not working, but also to sculpt his body into a perfect example of masculine beauty. "Oh God, yes, David," he purred back.

David had always been a big fan of phone sex, and Tim had noticed the phone bill usually contained a long list of calls to 900 numbers. "I can taste your cock in my mouth," he continued, his voice heavy with lust. "Doesn't it feel delicious?"

Tim wet his palm with his tongue and placed it on his penis, which jumped against the warmth of his hand. "Fuck, David, yes. Suck it baby, just the way I like it." He pulled his hand into a tight fist, moving it up and down the long shaft of his cock in ever-quickening movements.

David made slurping noises with his mouth and tongue, urging Tim on, cooing softly into his end of the line. Tim tossed his head back, trying hard to keep the phone cradled between his ear and shoulder blade. He was using his free hand to pinch his nipple, now swollen beneath the pressure of his forefinger and thumb. With a loud groan, he expelled his semen, which fell in large droplets onto his hand and down onto his upper thigh and knee.

"You taste so good, baby," David murmured from six thousand miles away. "I love the way you taste, especially after a workout."

Tim breathed an elongated sigh. "Please hurry home," he said, his voice thick with hunger and longing.

"I'll be with you before you know it."

Tim moaned in satisfaction. "I can't wait until then."

8

January 1994, Malaysia

The pyrotechnic expert had checked and rechecked the explosive canisters situated beneath the shoddily constructed bamboo pier. They had enough daylight for only one shot, and everything had to go perfectly, or the day—and half a million dollars—would be wasted. Everyone on the set knew that there was no money to waste; there was hardly enough money to finish the movie, and the director kept cutting corners in an effort to keep the film under budget.

Tim was standing on the bank of the Pahang River, inspecting the brackish, mosquito-infested waters below and wondering if he had received enough inoculations for all the diseases that ran amok in this godforsaken outpost. Two months in Malaysia had him pining for the more familiar comforts of home. Luckily, this would be the last day of filming, if the explosive finale went as planned.

It had taken some finagling on David's part, but he had managed to convince Talbot Grayson, the hotshot new director out of the United Kingdom, to place the future of his latest movie franchise in the hands of an untried talent such as Tim Race. He had absolutely no interest whatsoever in the fact that Tim was once on some silly American soap opera and had been nominated for a pretentious award: Could the guy kick ass while looking sexy covered in blood and sweat and holding a machete in his hand? Talbot had taken one look at Tim at their initial meeting in Hong Kong and known instantly he was the one. Tim needed a great deal of coaching, naturally. He had to study under a host of martial arts experts. He had to mold his body into a flawless, energy-efficient machine. To accomplish this feat, he practiced yoga each day, drank only purified water, and eliminated all dairy products, red meat, and liquor from his system. Within weeks, Tim looked and felt like a new man entirely. His body fat dropped below 5 percent and his skin had a radiant glow, purged of all the impurities that had collected within him during the course of his life.

Filming had been incredibly difficult. Cast and crew members were constantly coming down with bizarre ailments and injuries. Each day, the convoy of movie technicians, directors, camera people, and actors left the comforts of Kuala Lumpur in crowded minivans and RVs to return to the location shoot deep within the primeval Malay rain forest.

Despite all the hardships of filming, Tim thoroughly enjoyed his role as Winston Churchill Scanlon, a onetime member of a wealthy and powerful family who had turned his back on the family fortune to help people in desperate trouble. He was one part Robin Hood and one part James Bond, with a touch of Chuck Norris tossed in for good measure.

"Okay, places, everyone," Talbot shouted through the megaphone. "As you know, this is the final shot for the movie, so let's make sure we get it one hundred percent correct," he said in his crisp English accent.

As Tim's presence was not required in the scene, he joined Talbot on the raised platform that had been constructed to aid with the filming.

"So, Tim. How do you feel about the end of shooting for *Death Never Waits?* You think you could do another one of these things?" Talbot asked, not looking at Tim but concentrating on the upcoming scene.

"If this movie's a success, then I'm your man," Tim replied, catching the eye of one of the local Malaysian boys.

Several of the teenaged boys in the neighboring village had taken a liking to Tim, following him around like lost puppy dogs whenever he left his trailer. Each day they would offer to bring him fresh water or whatever he needed. Tim had taken one of the older boys, who had sworn in his broken English that he was eighteen, into his trailer and allowed the boy to give him a full-body massage. His skin still tingled when he thought of the massage and the little extra something the boy had given him. The young man saw Tim staring at him, and he bowed his head, smiling sweetly to reveal two rows of perfect white teeth. He then continued walking along the riverbank with the rest of his friends, who began teasing him noisily.

"This movie had better make some money. After all, I'm coming in well over a million bloody dollars under budget! Let's see the other wankers making this type of movie top that," Talbot said, before shouting again into the megaphone. "All right, everyone. Let's make this explosion rattle the earth to its core!"

"I certainly do miss you," Raina sighed. She had been on location in Australia for the past several months, filming a television miniseries based on a famous novel while her sitcom was on hiatus. "It's been so incredibly boring working in this dusty, outback hole-in-the-wall. Plus I've been desperately horny lately, with no prospects in sight. I have an idea. Since your birthday is a few days away and you're finished filming *Death Never Waits,* why don't you fly down to Sydney and we can have some fun?"

"That does sound wonderful. I could use a little downtime to rest and unwind before heading back to Los Angeles. I hope that David doesn't mind. It's been weeks since we've been together, and he may have already made plans for my birthday."

Tim could almost hear the sound of Raina's teeth grinding over the crackle and hiss of static on the line. "For crying out loud, Tim. Do you think you can possibly wean yourself away from David for just a little while? The two of you don't always have to be attached at the hip, you know."

Tim knew that Raina was more than a little jealous of his relationship with David, and vice versa. It perturbed him that he felt he was being disloyal to one while spending time with the other.

"I promise I will meet you in Sydney. How about the day after tomorrow?"

Raina's voice brightened considerably. "Hooray! I cannot wait until then!"

On Tim's twenty-third birthday, Raina escorted him for a night on the town. Sydney is a cosmopolitan, liberal city, as exciting and culturally rich as it is beautiful. Raina had booked them a suite in a de-luxe hotel with expansive views of the famous Opera House and the Sydney Harbour Bridge, which looked a bit like a glittering coat hanger spanning the breathtaking bay.

In celebration of his birthday, Raina had made plans to take Tim to the city's Kings Cross, a district full of tony restaurants, bars, and clubs, a small-scale, more laid-back version of New York's Times Square or London's Piccadilly Circus. On a side street off Darlinghurst Road, they entered a strip joint called the Mappa Tassie, which was Australian slang for "map of Tasmania," a colloquialism for the va-gina.

"I don't get the name," Tim said over the pounding beat of a Kylie Minogue dance hit.

"Map of Tasmania," Raina explained. "You know, the little trian-gular-shaped island off the southern coast of Australia?" She formed a triangle with her forefingers and thumbs.

"Oh, now I get it," Tim lied. A trio of topless women were now dancing on the stage, all wearing leather chaps and cowboy boots with spurs, a six-gun hanging jauntily from each of their holsters.

"Let's head next door." Raina nudged Tim with her elbow. "I be-lieve you will like the ambiance over there far better," she added.

The club next door was appropriately named Didgeridoos, which, as it turned out, was Aussie slang for the penis. As they entered the club through a darkened archway, Tim noticed that it was full of mainly men, with a smattering of female faces blended in the mix. Tim was not overly concerned with being recognized; it would be months before his movie premiered, and the episodes of *The Drifting Clouds* currently being broadcast in Australia were several years be-hind those seen in the States, before Tim had joined the cast.

Dance music began to pipe through the loudspeakers, and the lights suddenly dimmed. A hush fell over the crowd before the stage curtain opened up. A group of five muscular men wearing identical, tight, black leather pants and white vests stood side by side. As the beat of the music increased, each man began to move in coordinated dance steps, slowly removing each article of clothing, to the delight of the rowdy audience.

"What did I tell you about Australian men?" Raina crowed excitedly over the din of noise. "They are so amazingly sexy!"

Tim had to agree as he surveyed the abundant smorgasbord of male pulchritude before him. The catcalls from the male and female patrons grew more intense until each man was clad in only a tiny black leather thong, bulging to capacity.

Tim's attention was focused on the golden blond in the middle, who looked as if he had stepped out of a mold cast from an ancient Greek statue.

Raina noticed where his eyes had settled. "His name is Caleb. He's nineteen and a professional surfer who grew up on Bondi Beach. Isn't he absolutely dreamy?"

"And just how do you know so much about the guy?" Tim asked.

Raina batted her curled eyelashes at Tim. "He's your birthday present. Happy birthday, baby!"

"No worries," Caleb said in his unmistakable Australian accent after Raina informed him they did not have any Fosters beer. "I'll drink whatever you got around."

Raina handed him a small can of a local brew she found in the hotel suite's miniature refrigerator. "So, Caleb. You are a professional surfer as well as an exotic dancer?"

"Yeah," he said, running a hand through his curly, shoulder-length hair that was still damp from the shower he had taken before leaving the club. His eyes were a mesmerizing bluish-green, the color of the waters surrounding the Great Barrier Reef, which looked even more striking set against his golden-bronze tan. He was now wearing a slightly dingy T-shirt, stained by the ocean surf, and baggy shorts, beach sandals on his large feet. "The surfing doesn't pay too much, unless you have a corporate sponsor. I make a lot more money dancing at the clubs."

He popped the top to the beer can and took a swig. "Cheers, mate. You two really big stars over in America?"

"I wouldn't say big stars," Tim answered, speaking for the first time since they had arrived back at the hotel.

"That's real cool. I always wanted to act in the movies or on television. The closest I ever got was when they were filming some movie up in Surfers Paradise in Queensland and they got a shot of me riding a killer wave way off in the distance."

"Sounds interesting. Well, you do know the reason why we brought you here, don't you?" Raina questioned, wanting to cut to the chase.

Caleb grinned sheepishly. "Yeah. I think I know, anyway. You guys looking for a little three-way action, correct?"

"That depends," Raina replied, studying Tim's facial expression, which did not change. "Have you ever been with a man before?"

"Sure. I mean, I'm not a bleedin' poofter or anything, but most beach bums in Australia have done it with a guy before, whether they admit it or not." He directed his gaze at Tim. "I like the way you look, mate. A right good-looking Yank, you are."

"Thank you," Tim said quietly. He wasn't altogether comfortable with the way things were turning out. Something about the situation just didn't feel right to him. The variables of the equation seemed somehow out of sequence: Raina was attracted to Tim, who was attracted to the Aussie hunk, who was attracted to them both. The missing element, he concluded, was his physical attraction to Raina.

"Very well then. Shall we proceed?" She had moved over to the bed.

Caleb stood up from the chair and stretched his arms behind his head. "Right on, then. Who's first?" he inquired, pulling the T-shirt over his head to reveal his perfectly sculpted chest and abdomen. He stepped out of his baggy shorts and kicked his sandals aside.

Both Tim and Raina admired his uncircumcised penis, long and veiny, as it began to swell. It was far too heavy to reach a full vertical erection, so it dangled impressively between his powerfully muscular legs.

"Tim, seeing that today is your birthday, I think you deserve the honors," Raina offered graciously, always the perfect hostess.

There was a pause before Tim responded. "That's all right. Ladies first. I think I would like to watch the two of you together for a while."

A brief look of panic crossed her face. She took a deep breath.

"Fair enough. Let's begin." She fumbled with the top buttons on her chamois-cloth blouse before pulling it over her head. Caleb stood behind her and undid the clasp on her bra, allowing it to fall to the floor, exposing her full, natural breasts. Caleb cupped both breasts in his hands as he kissed the back of her neck.

"You're a sexy sheila," Caleb murmured wetly into her ear, his voice laced with macho Australian bravado.

Raina was looking at Tim, a plaintive expression on her face, as if she was suddenly aware that this entire scene had been a colossal mistake. Caleb, swept up in his own passion, failed to notice her reticence when he lifted her lithe body up and placed her softly onto the bed.

"Just remember, bloke. You're next in line," he said boastfully to Tim, pulling down Raina's Capri pants. Curiously, he hooked his pinkie finger into the tiny opening of her navel, the odd sensation causing Raina to shiver in discomfort. He bent down to kiss her stomach, his tongue forming a glistening trail up to the fold between her breasts. Raina's eyes were closed as he twisted the elastic band of her panties around both of his thumbs and gently tugged them downward, past her knees and to her ankles. He placed his hand on her blonde pubic mound and parted her gently with two fingers, exploring further until he discovered her clitoris.

Tim watched on, somewhere between lust and revulsion. *This isn't really what Raina wants,* he thought. *I don't want this either . . .*

Abruptly, Raina sat up on the bed, bringing Caleb's expert manipulation to a sudden halt.

"I'm sorry," she whispered. "I can't go through with this."

Caleb looked up at her quizzically. "Am I not doing it right?" he asked, his pride a little bruised.

"It's not you at all," Raina said, pulling her blouse back over her head and jumping back into her pants. "Again, I'm sorry. I was wrong to have approached you." She reached into her purse and pulled out a handful of Australian dollars, which was all of the cash that she had on her.

Caleb accepted the money, considerably put off and flustered by the situation. "No worries," he said nonchalantly in his singsong voice.

He looked over at Tim. "I suppose it's a no-go with you, too?"

Tim nodded his head.

"Yanks," he muttered with insolence before he finished putting his clothes back on, leaving the room without another word.

They didn't speak for the longest while. They both sat on the bed, the silence broken only by Raina's occasional sniffles and the distant sound of the street traffic outside.

"I am so sorry, Tim," she apologized after several minutes had passed. "For some insane reason, I thought that this would bring us closer together. I don't know what I was thinking."

"You don't have to apologize to me, Raina. You just got in a little over your head, that's all." Tim reached over and touched her cheek, which felt flushed, from embarrassment or from fear or both.

"You don't understand. It's you that I want, as stupid and ridiculous and pathetic as that may sound." She finally let go of her tears, and they flowed hotly down her cheeks in wide rivulets.

Tim pulled her against him and held her tightly. "But I do love you so. I always will."

"Just not in the way that I want you to love me," she cried.

"I love you in the only way that truly matters," Tim said, his own tears falling freely onto Raina's, joining together to form a bitter torrent.

9

London is just as I imagined it would be, Tim thought, staring out the window of the regal-looking taxicab as it threaded its way through the bumper-to-bumper traffic on Oxford Street. *The city is so very sophisticated and refined.*

For certain, the British capital had more than its fair share of instantly recognizable landmarks and monuments, beautiful parks, impressive palaces, imperial museums, and world-famous department stores.

David watched the thrill on Tim's face at visiting London for the first time, contentment sparkling in his eyes. He enjoyed experiencing the excitement of life vicariously through Tim; it somehow made him feel years younger.

The two were in London to attend the world premiere of *Death Never Waits.* They had just come from having afternoon tea at Talbot Grayson's beautiful Georgian estate on Eaton Square. The London critics had been raving in advance about the film and about Tim's raw and honest performance in it. The scuttlebutt sounding from both sides of the Atlantic was that the film was destined to be a box-office smash. The studio was paying the expense of the publicity junket to Great Britain, which included round-trip tickets for Tim and David to London via the supersonic Concorde, confident that the movie would earn back the cost plus the film's rather modest budget.

"I hope that Raina will make it in time for the premiere," Tim said, watching the passing parade of fashionable Londoners, dressed warmly to fight off the damp, winter chill.

"I'm sure she'll be here. I haven't been able to find her much work since the cancellation of *Ain't That a Shame?* I blame the stupid network for tinkering with the show's schedule. It could easily have gone on another two or three seasons. At least she'll be receiving residual checks from the syndication deal. She's wanted for years to come to

London to try her hand at theater in the West End. There's absolutely no money in it, of course, but it will look great on her résumé."

Since the incident in Australia, Tim and Raina had bonded even further. Raina now accepted the fact that Tim could not offer her the physical love that she needed, but they remained steadfast, loyal friends. In many ways, she was his anchor to the real world, which he often lost sight of in the heady, whirlwind existence his life had recently become.

"I knew that you would come," Tim said, rushing to give Raina a warm, welcoming embrace.

She had been waiting for an hour in the lobby of the venerable Dorchester Hotel for Tim and David to arrive. "I was cutting it close. I had an audition for a movie yesterday in New York, but I managed to catch a flight out to Heathrow last night, so here I am."

She looked tired and jet-lagged, but Tim knew that an hour with a makeup artist and hairstylist would have her looking smashing in plenty of time for the premiere. "You don't know how happy I am to see you here," Tim said. "It wouldn't have felt right not having you with me today."

David cleared his throat. "So, Raina, how did the audition go for that movie, anyway? I really think it is time for you to make a move to meatier acting roles."

"I think it went pretty well, but you know how that goes. I was a little nervous, naturally, so I guess we'll have to see."

"You'll get the part," Tim assured. She was far too talented an actress to remain unemployed for very long.

"Let's hope," she said, crossing her fingers before noticing that she was in dire need of a manicure. "Dear Lord, get me to a salon, but quick!"

At the star-studded premiere of *Death Never Waits,* it was Tim's star that sparkled brightest of all in the cold London night. The paparazzi waited three deep outside the Odeon Theatre in Leicester Square, desperate to snap photographs that would be purchased by the infamous British tabloids. Tim, fetching in his tailored Ralph Lauren suit, and Raina, a knockout in a flowing Oscar de la Renta gown, wowed the crowd with their attractiveness and smiling charm. In attendance were a handful of diplomats and other dignitaries, including several low-rent members of the extended Royal Family, always eager for a convenient photo-op to get their pictures in the papers.

Tim sat in the darkened theater, watching himself on the big screen, feeling rather like the proverbial little fish in a tremendously large pond. *Do they like me?* a nagging little voice in his mind asked. *Am I any good?*

At the movie's end, the lights went back on in the theater. Tim closed his eyes briefly and held his breath. Suddenly, the sound of applause erupted from all around him. He opened his eyes to discover both David and Raina, along with the entire audience, standing in ovation. With his knees shaking, Tim finally managed to rise and join in the applause.

"A trilogy, that's what the studio is aiming for," Talbot Grayson said, pausing to take a bite of his steak tartare. The sight of the raw meat quivering on Talbot's plate made Tim feel a bit queasy. Talbot, Tim, and David had met at a quaint, English-style steak house near the La Brea Tar Pits for an afternoon of power brokering. "Your fee has increased significantly, I would imagine."

David spoke for Tim. "In light of *Death Never Waits'* incredible success around the world, I would have to say yes to that."

Tim had been paid only $50,000 for his first movie, which was a mere pittance when compared with how much the film had grossed. In the seven months since the movie had been released in the theaters, the film had brought in more than $200 million internationally, making it one of the most successful motion pictures of all time.

"I see. What sort of range would we be talking about here?" Talbot asked with his typical British reserve.

"Five million, up front. Plus five percent of worldwide net receipts, including video sales and rentals," David drilled off quickly, in an attempt to make it sound like the best conceivable offer.

"*Cor!* That's pretty steep, old chap. But I think the studio will be willing to accept those conditions."

Like that, the deal was set, and Tim did not have to say a single word.

A few days later, Tim and Raina were enjoying the sun on the balcony of her bright and airy new condo, high above the smog and noise in the Hollywood Hills. Tim had already received the hastily written script for his next movie, the imaginatively titled *Death Never Smiles*. He was reading the entertainment section of the newspaper while Raina perused the horoscopes.

"My horoscope sucks," she said indignantly, flipping the newspaper page over. "It never pertains to anything about me. I find 'Hints from Heloise' applying more to my life these days," she said, noticing several handprint smudges on the French doors leading to the balcony.

Tim looked up from the article he had been reading about the genius of Steven Spielberg. "What does my horoscope say, just out of curiosity?"

"You're a Capricorn, the goat, right? Let's see . . . 'Be ready to travel, visit others and explore new horizons. Now is the time for your star to shine.' Really, now? Isn't that what they all say?"

Time for my star to shine, Tim thought to himself. *Hell, Tim Race's star is just about to go supernova!*

BOOK TWO:
TWILIGHT IN BALBOA PARK

10

"Muévete, maricon," snarled the scrawny young man with the buck-teeth and cystic acne.

Jaime Adame de Valdivias bristled at the man's nasty epithet. He had always hated the word *maricon,* which was the Spanish equivalent of the English word *faggot.*

Jaime glared at the man. He knew that the man was jealous because Jaime could attract the better-looking and better-paying clients that cruised the perimeter of San Diego's beautiful Balboa Park. The unpleasant man was only twenty-two years old but looked far older because he was a huffer who was addicted to sniffing solvents and paint thinner on a daily basis. The area was littered with such people. He usually attracted only the deviant trolls that hit the park in droves after dark each night. Jaime had learned early on to avoid the trolls like the plague, which was wise if you valued your own life.

Jaime had been standing peacefully along the railing of Cabrillo Bridge, which was the most popular entryway into the park, watching the sun set and minding his own business.

"Chinga tu madre," Jaime hissed back, retaliating with the worst slur you could hand to someone of Hispanic heritage: *Fuck your mother.*

The young man curled his face into a foul grimace before he pushed his way past Jaime, entering the park.

Jaime had by now become quite familiar with the way life worked out on the streets. As in most societies, there was a strict hierarchy here, a natural pecking order. He had been living his life on the streets for the past eight months, and if you didn't learn fast, you were doomed.

He was tall for a Mexican, many of his gringo johns would often tell him. At the age of eighteen, he had finally sprouted three inches during the course of the summer. Dressed in a plain white T-shirt and loose-fitting blue jeans, he was reed thin, just on the verge of emaciation, but his legs and arms were still muscular and taut. Occasionally, one of the men who picked him up would buy him a burger and some fries. More often than not, however, he was left to his own devices when it came to scrounging up something to eat. It wasn't overly difficult, as people were constantly throwing away half-eaten plates of food while enjoying the many diversions the park offered to the public. His dark, straight hair had grown long over the past several months and now rested on his broad shoulders. His hair was clean and smelled of apple-scented hand soap; even though he lived on the street, he still managed to maintain good personal hygiene by using the park's well-stocked bathrooms. His skin had the wonderful cinnamon cast that displayed his rich Aztec ancestry. He was a true mestizo, of the mixed blood of the indigenous Mexican people and the Spanish conquistadors who had decimated the land and enslaved its inhabitants centuries before.

At one time, Jaime had had a good life. Born into a poor but hardworking family in a tiny village in the state of Guanajuato, he had spent his idyllic childhood days playing near the many silver mines that were scattered throughout the hills of central Mexico. Joel, his father, had worked in the silver mines along with Jaime's uncles and his eldest brother, Mario. Jaime's mother, Lorena, had taken care of him and his seven other brothers and sisters. They had lived in a tiny, dirt-floored hut without running water, located on the outskirts of the village. Though they had little money, the household was full of love, laughter, and joy, for poverty is far more common in Mexico than misery. Each day Jaime, along with one of his brothers or sisters, would trek into the village a mile or so away to visit the town's communal well. They would often stop and take baths or play in the water basin, never thinking twice that this was the town's main fresh water supply. They would then carry the heavy buckets full of water home for their mother to do the cooking and washing.

Later on, after the silver mines had been stripped of all of their rich ore, times became quite difficult for the townspeople. There was no more work in the tiny village. Jaime's father heard that there was work to be found in the historic town of San Miguel de Allende, several hundred miles away. He packed up the family's meager belongings and made the move to San Miguel. In the magical city, full of narrow, cobbled, and hilly streets, colorfully painted bougainvillea-draped walls, and ornate churches, Jaime's father found employment as a caretaker in a hotel that had been a sixteenth-century monastery. His mother worked as a maid for one of the many American expatriate families who lived in the hidden colonial jewel of San Miguel de Allende. Jaime flourished, earning the odd peso by running errands for the wealthy expatriates, who doted on him and his brothers and sisters. He began picking up quite a bit of the English language and did well in his studies at school. He had always been a bright boy, his mother would say with great pride.

One early autumn day, Jaime's father had told his mother he was not feeling very well, but that he was going to report to work at the hotel as usual. Jaime, who was a growing sixteen-year-old at the time, had still been attending school. When he arrived back at the home with his five younger brothers and sisters in tow, he found his mother alone and crying in the kitchen, where she had been spent half of the day preparing tamales for the family's dinner.

"Mama," he had asked her softly, "why are you crying?"

She had looked at him, her eyes red, before holding the crucifix worn around her neck up to her lips and giving it a tender kiss. "It is your papa, my son. He has died and gone to heaven."

His father had died of a massive heart attack while at work. Several of his co-workers were kind enough to bring his body back to the house. He now lay silent on the soft mattress that he had stuffed himself from gathered chicken feathers. His mother took his only good suit out of the closet and, with Jaime's help, dressed his rigid body. As there was no money for a proper funeral, it fell upon Jaime and his brother Mario to dig a grave for their father. They dug the grave in a small cemetery used by the town's *campesinos*—peasants—situated on a hill overlooking the Parroquia, the majestic and fantastical gothic cathedral carved from pink sandstone that dominated the town's skyline. He was laid to rest that very evening, the entire family carrying homemade candles and torches to make their way up the hill in the night. The family's priest officiated, Lorena and her eight children weeping in the dark.

The day after the funeral, Lorena had turned to Jaime. "I will be depending on you for many things now, *mi hijo*. Your brother Mario has a wife and children of his own to care for, so you are the next-to-eldest son. You must be the man of the house now."

"Yes, Mother," he replied dutifully, as she pulled him to her chest.

The following day, Jaime stopped attending school. It was now his duty to make sure his brothers and sisters were taken care of, so there would be no more time for his education.

"Do not worry, Mama. We will be fine. Our family is strong," he had reassured her.

"I know that, *mi amor*," she said to him lovingly.

It was then that Jaime decided to heed the call to leave for America. His brother Mario was planning on leaving for the States within the next several months. He had paid a man more than ten thousand pesos to be transported illegally into the country. The trip would be long, uncomfortable, and fraught with danger. Jaime knew that in order to help his family, he would have to make the voyage as well.

When he told his mother of his plans, she stared back at him in a pained, understanding way. "I knew this day would come," she whispered, hugging him close. *"Vaya con dios, mi hijo,"* she said to him tearfully, as untold thousands of mothers had told their sons throughout the long and turbulent history of Mexico.

On el Día de los Muertos, the day families all across Mexico remember their deceased loved ones, the entire family visited the gravesite of their lost husband and father. Jaime's mother had packed a wicker basket full of delicious food and drink. The children feasted on yummy sugar candies fashioned in the shapes of skeletons and coffins. They sat on blankets and ate their food amidst the simple tombstones, the cemetery full of families enjoying the warm and sunny November day. The celebration was not a somber one, for death in the Mexican culture is viewed not as an ending, but rather as the beginning of a wonderful and joyous new existence.

Jaime and his brother spent Christmas Day with their family. They attended midnight Mass together and prayed to the Virgin of Guadalupe for Jaime and Mario's safe passage into America. They left the day after Christmas, packing what clothes they could into tattered knapsacks. Their mother had prepared them each a care package, full of tacos, *gorditas con chicharrones,* and *dulces de tamarindo,* a favorite candy of Jaime's.

With tears in her eyes, Lorena said good-bye to her two strong and handsome sons. "May God bless you both and keep you safe on your journey to America," she told them, before pulling each of them into an embrace and handing them their care packages, wrapped in multi-colored, hand-sewn serapes. She then handed Jaime the ten thousand pesos it would cost for the journey.

"We will be fine, Mama," Jaime said confidently. "Once we find jobs in America, we will send money back home for you and my brothers and sisters."

After the tearful exchange of good-byes, the Volkswagen minibus swerved its way through the winding streets of San Miguel before heading north through the bleak and barren desert that stretched on into seeming infinity. Ten people were packed into the back of the hot and smelly minibus, its grimy windows hidden behind ugly, paisley curtains that looked as if they had not been washed since the early 1970s. The only time the minibus stopped was to refuel. Several of the other passengers had not taken baths, and the stench began to grow overpowering to Jaime, who held his breath for long intervals to avoid becoming sick to his stomach. An older gentleman who sat beside Mario had fallen ill, but the driver would not stop to let him out, until he finally vomited into his already soiled New York Mets baseball cap, the retching noises echoing off the walls of the van. Jaime found himself becoming more nauseated and more claustrophobic by the second. The ride was beginning to feel interminable to him, the body odor now mingling with the acrid smell of vomit.

Throughout the day and night, the unbearable voyage continued. There were three men who alternated driving so there would be no need to stop and rest during the night. Into the next morning, the vehicle rattled and shook its way forward, the landscape of enormous cacti and endless desert rushing by at top speed.

Jaime lost count of the hours. He had no appetite, so he shared his food with the elderly gentleman who had been so sick the day before.

To pass the time, the passengers sang Mexican folk songs and told jokes, laughing in order to keep from crying.

Finally, the Volkswagen neared the border. The passengers would be transported to a location a few miles outside of Tijuana, where they would be escorted across the border. They would have to wait until sundown before attempting the crossing, as border control agents always heavily patrolled the region during the day.

The Volkswagen parked in an isolated area and the passengers waited for nightfall. Jaime began to feel nervous tension building within him at the thought of crossing the border. It was a risky procedure, as literally hundreds of *mojados*—illegal immigrants—were caught crossing the border each day and deported back to Mexico.

After dark, one of the men who had arranged the trip told everyone to get out of the van. They would be led to an area where it should be relatively safe to cross into the country. They made their way through the night, risking scorpion stings and rattlesnake bites every step of the way. Since the border was not marked, the guides would have to use landmarks to tell whether they were in the United States. Suddenly, a helicopter buzzed overhead, searchlights flooding the desert. The whir of all-terrain truck engines was followed by shouts in English. They had been spotted! The border agents used thermal imaging cameras that could see anything that moved in the dark of night. One of the guides yelled for them all to disperse. Jaime turned to look for Mario, but he was already running in the opposite direction. There was no time to switch gears. Flight instinct immediately kicked in, adrenaline coursing throughout Jaime's body. He ran as fast and as hard as he could, the dust from the ground pelting him in the face and scratching at his eyes. On and on he ran, until the sounds of the helicopter and trucks began to fade and he realized that he was alone in the night.

Disoriented and exhausted, he paused to catch his breath. He had no clue where he was. Far off in the distance, he saw the sparkle of city lights. He wandered into the darkness, making his way toward the beacon of lights and to freedom. He prayed that Mario had escaped and that he would find him one day.

It took him several hours to reach the city. By the time he did, the sun was rising over San Diego. He had done it! He had made it safely across the border. What he had to do next, he did not know, but at least he was here, in America. He managed to hitch a ride with a fellow Mexican national driving a battered Buick, who dropped him off on Sixth Avenue in downtown San Diego before continuing on his way.

An inner compass guided him to the entrance of Balboa Park. The cantilevered bridge going into the park reminded him of the Roman-style aqueduct he had seen as a child during a visit with his family to the city of Querétaro in Mexico. The Museum of Man's two-hundred-foot bell tower and lavishly tiled central dome also reminded him of home.

It was in the splendid surroundings of Balboa Park that Jaime began to learn the harsh realities of his new life. Separated from his loving family, he learned that life in America was not always so ideal and perfect. He discovered that sex can sometimes be the only thing of value one has in this world, and that certain men are more than willing to pay for it.

It's time to get to work, Jaime thought as he watched the setting sun cast eerie shadows across the California Tower, which had just chimed the Westminster bells marking the quarter of the hour. He entered the park through the neoclassical archway of the West Gate as he did every night, never knowing what the capricious fates might have in store for him.

⭐ 11

Tim revved the engine of the Mercedes SLK 320 while waiting for the traffic light to turn green. Hitting San Diego just at sunset, he was more than ready to be out on the prowl. The billboards tempting the omnipresent tourists to visit Balboa Park and the San Diego Zoo piqued his interest. Tim followed the abundant signs that guided the way to the park.

He pulled up to the West Gate just as a large group of elderly lawn bowlers, clad in white from head to toe, were leaving the park. It suddenly occurred to him that he might be recognized, so he pulled a cap out of the glove box and placed it on his head, pulling the bill over his eyes.

Eager to step out of the car and to move his legs after the long drive, he quickly found a parking space. The park was full of many families, but he immediately saw that the area was also very cruisey. A mixture of men, both young and old, was milling about and checking out the scene along the El Prado thoroughfare. Not wanting to look overly conspicuous, Tim put his sunglasses back on, since there was still a glimmer of sunlight left.

Tim walked swiftly, passing the lovely Alcazar Garden, full of fragrant flowers in bloom, before stopping briefly to watch a group of children playing in the Spanish-tiled fountain in the Plaza de Panama. He continued on, passing stately date palms, coastal live oaks, and eucalyptus trees, which filled the air with their distinctive scent. At the House of Hospitality, he noticed the young Hispanic man standing in front of the lily pond reflecting pool situated between the lattice-structured botanical gardens and the Casa de Balboa. From his stance and body language, Tim could instantly tell that he was a street hustler. He was looking toward the House of Hospitality, wearing a T-shirt and jeans, his hands deep in his pockets, a faded knapsack resting at his feet. Tim lifted his sunglasses a few millimeters as he walked by the young man. Their eyes locked for a brief second. Tim smiled at him, which the man acknowledged with an almost undetectable nod of his head. Tim felt a lurch in his pants. It had been a while since he had had sex, and he needed to have some human contact, particularly after his nightmarish ordeal at the detox clinic. He desperately needed an outlet for sexual release. Tim continued walking but turned his head back to look again at the handsome young man, who was staring after him. Tim turned around in front of the east side of the Casa del Prado, the tourists gawking at the complex carved tableau and hieroglyphics-inscribed cartouche of the building's exterior from Balboa Plaza. The young man had crossed the street and was now standing beneath the Romanesque colonnade connecting the House of Hospitality and the Casa de Balboa.

Tim paused and waited for a chattering family of Japanese tourists to walk by before crossing over the walkway to where the Hispanic man now stood, observing him closely with his dark chocolate-colored eyes with the long, curled lashes.

"Do you speak English?" Tim asked, lowering his sunglasses to expose his own sparkling emerald-green eyes. There didn't appear to be any recognition there.

"Yes, I can speak some English," Jaime responded in a soft lilt, his hands still buried deep within his jean pockets.

"Great. Are you . . . working tonight?" Tim asked carefully, monitoring the man's movements and expressions while quickly surveying the area. The last thing he needed was to fall into some sting operation.

"Yes, I'm working. What are you looking for tonight?"

Tim stared blankly at the man. He had never done this sort of thing before, so he was unsure of the exact protocol of the situation. "Hmmm, whatever you are offering," he finally said.

"Okay. It will cost you though. You got a place to go do it?"

Tim stared deep into the hustler's eyes. They were so young and innocent, it was hard to believe that he was even here, selling his body to strangers for money. Tim suddenly felt a pang of guilt, but the stirrings in his pants urged him onward.

"Sure. We can go to a hotel nearby. Someplace nice and clean. That sound good to you?"

Jaime nodded his head. "You got a car?"

"Yes, I do. Follow me," Tim replied. He pulled his sunglasses back up over his eyes and turned around to inspect the scene once again.

There were large groups of families and tourists, enjoying twilight in Balboa Park and not paying any attention to him and the street hustler. Tim led the way back to his Mercedes parked at Plaza de Panama. Jaime followed several paces behind, for he knew that the police were continuously patrolling the park in an effort to weed out the prostitutes and undesirables. There had been a public outcry in San Diego several years before after a prime-time network news program did an exposé on the street hustlers of Balboa Park and the unscrupulous men who preyed upon them. Still, the police couldn't keep all of the hustlers out of the park, for they numbered in the thousands, and as soon as some were arrested and deported back to Mexico or other Latin American countries, more arrived to replace them.

Once they arrived back at Tim's car, he unlocked the doors using his remote. The two got into the car, and Jaime marveled at the plush interior of the automobile. Now there was the dilemma of where to go. Usually when Tim was in San Diego, he stayed at the historic, wood-structured Hotel del Coronado located right on the beach. That was certainly not an option in this case. He would have to choose a nondescript motel nearby, one that accepted cash and did not ask any questions.

As if reading Tim's thoughts, Jaime spoke again. "There's a cheap motel just down the road a mile or so. That's where a lot of men take me."

Tim glanced over at the handsome young man as they exited the park. "What's your name, by the way?" he asked.

"Jaime," was his response. "And what is your name?"

"Tim," he said, before realizing that he probably shouldn't have used his real name. "So, how much do you charge for this sort of thing?"

"I guess we can talk business now. I'm sure you're not a cop now. No cop would be driving this car," Jaime said with a smile.

"No, I'm not a cop," Tim reassured him. "Is this the motel up ahead?"

"Yes. The manager knows me, but he don't care as long as you tip him a twenty or something. He'll just look the other way."

Tim maneuvered the Mercedes into the darkened parking lot. He saw a few other young Hispanic men standing outside one of the rooms. One of them recognized Jaime and waved. Tim parked in front of the shabby office with its bright red neon sign. Inside, Tim could see a fat man standing at the front desk, wearing a flannel shirt and eating a hamburger.

"I'll be right back," he told Jaime before stepping out of the car and removing his cap and sunglasses. He quickly checked his billfold to make sure he had enough cash on him. He certainly wasn't about to use his credit card to reserve the room for the night. The sign above the office stated that rooms were twenty-five dollars per night. Fortunately, he had more than enough cash on him to foot the bill.

The jingling bells hanging on the office door heralded his arrival. The fat man looked up briefly from his comic book before continuing on with his reading. Drops of grease from his hamburger were falling onto the pages.

"Excuse me. Do you have any vacancies?" Tim asked.

The man looked up again, his rheumy eyes washing unseeingly over Tim's face. "That's what the sign says out front, don't it, bud?" he said with a sardonic smirk on his ruddy, plump face.

"Very well," Tim said, ignoring the man's sarcasm. "I'd like to rent a room for tonight."

The man closed the comic book. "You gonna need the room the whole night? Usually, most of the guys that come here with boys only need the room a few hours."

Tim felt his face grow hot. "Yes, I need the room for the entire night," he said, his brow furrowing in displeasure. He was not accustomed to dealing with unpleasant people; for the past decade, he had always had the buffer of agents and publicists to protect him from such distasteful things.

"Okay, then. That's fifty bucks, including a gratuity for me, just to keep my mouth shut." The man took another bite of his burger, several crumbs of meat and bread sticking to his lips and chin.

Tim handed him a fifty-dollar bill without saying another word. The man gave him the key to the room and chuckled fiendishly as he left the office. Tim motioned to Jaime, who opened the door to the car and followed him up the stairs to the motel room.

Tim inserted the key into the tarnished doorknob. He flipped on the light switch and inspected the ragged furnishings. The floor was carpeted in pea-green shag, which matched the paper-thin bedspread and curtains. It certainly was not the Ritz, but it would do for what Tim had in mind.

Jaime stood in front of the radiator, looking out the window onto the parking lot. "Would you like to wash up first?" Tim asked him.

Jaime turned around to look at him. "That would be nice," he said. He excused himself politely as he walked past Tim in the cramped quarters and entered the closet-sized bathroom. Luckily, there was a stand-up shower in the bathroom.

Tim sat down on the bed and waited for Jaime to finish taking a shower. There was a magazine rack by the bed, and Tim sifted through the old copies. There was a back issue of *Vanity Fair* with Tim on the cover, along with Tobey Maguire and Leonardo DiCaprio, from a year ago. Tim remembered how fun the photo shoot in New York had been, with Tobey and Leo joking around, the best of friends. Tim made sure to conceal the magazine in the drawer of the nightstand, placing it face down beneath the copy of the King James Bible.

Ten minutes later, Jaime emerged from his shower, his hair glistening with moisture. He had put his T-shirt and jeans back on, but he was barefoot. Tim caught his breath as he looked at this beautiful young man before him. He coughed to clear his throat.

"So, you never told me how much you charge," he said as Jaime stared down at his feet shyly.

"Depends on what you want. A blow job is usually twenty, but it's sixty for the full package," he answered, not looking into Tim's eyes.

"I guess I'll take the full package then," he said as he felt his penis stiffen. "Did you bring any protection with you?"

Jaime nodded his head. He reached into his pocket and pulled out a handful of condoms of varying sizes, textures, and colors. "I always keep some of these with me. Just to be safe. I don't want to get *SIDA*—AIDS."

"Thanks," Tim said quietly as he took one of the brightly colored packets. "I guess we should get on with it, then."

Jaime nodded again. Without a word, he pulled the T-shirt over his head, revealing his thin but tightly muscled torso and natural six-pack. The skin on his chest and upper arms was a slight shade lighter than on his lower arms, neck, and face. His pectoral muscles were neatly compacted and his hardened nipples resembled two miniature rosebuds against the darkness of his chest, where there was not a trace of body hair to be found. He unzipped his baggy jeans and let them drop to his ankles. Jaime was not wearing any underwear, and his penis was already erect and throbbing gently against the rippled muscles of his abdomen.

Tim breathed in sharply as he took in the sight of Jaime's delectably youthful body. He beckoned him to join him on the bed, which creaked and moaned under the weight of both of their bodies. Jaime had a distant, detached look on his face as Tim ran his hand across his chest, tweaking each nipple delicately before allowing his hand to sink further, across the hard grooves of his abdominal muscles. Standing up, Tim undid the top button of his Van Heusen gabardine trousers and carefully unzipped them before stuffing his free hand down the front and feeling the hardness of his cock, begging to be freed. Tim reached over and pulled Jaime's legs up onto the bed. Assiduously, he removed his own shoes and socks before he pulled down his pants and undid the buttons of his shirt, tossing it to the floor, so he too was completely naked.

Once Tim was on the bed again, Jaime sat up. Wordlessly, he bent forward and gripped the swollen head of Tim's cock in both of his gentle hands. Tim flinched from the sudden contact before easing into the sublime sensation, Jaime rubbing the aching head between the palms of his hands. Tim arched his back a few degrees and moaned his approval. Jaime deftly continued with his exquisite torment before angling his face downward. He began to lick the tightening flesh of Tim's scrotum, batting the sac playfully with his tongue until it swayed back and forth, as he continued to manipulate his cock with his skillful hands. With a sudden motion, Jaime took the tumescent tip of the cock into his mouth.

Tim gasped noisily at the intensity of the sensation. Whereas Jaime had seemed shy and modest when he was speaking with him moments before, he was now confident and in control as he sucked the length of Tim's dick deeply into his mouth, his tongue tapping and massaging the bottom of the engorged head. Jaime's innocent eyes now exhibited the jaded look he had earned from his eight months of living on the street. This was his job, his livelihood, and he was going to give it his all. Tim gripped the back of his neck, forcibly moving his face downward, until Jaime's nose was level with his navel, his nostrils buried into the patch of fine dark blond hair that trailed down to his groin. He twisted his face from side to side, continuing to pull the cock into the sealed vacuum of his mouth. Tim reached down with his hand and traced the outline of Jaime's upper lip with his thumb, watching in fascination as his penis slid in and out of his expert mouth.

The unbearable pleasure began to build deep within Tim. He gingerly tapped Jaime on the back of his neck to let him know it was time to try something different. With a knowing look in his eyes, Jaime released the pulsating penis from his mouth, the tight seal releasing with a loud *pop*. Tim took the condom package that had been resting on the pillow and opened it, extracting the lubricated rubber. He searched Jaime's eyes, which now looked up at him with a sense of ease and comfort. Tim placed the condom on his straining cock, instructing Jaime to lie on his back against the mattress. He did as he was told and watched Tim direct his stalwart erection toward Jaime's anus, pulling his legs up and resting his feet on Tim's shoulders.

Tim guided himself slowly into the warm, accepting aperture. He examined Jaime's face, making sure he was not going too forcibly. Jaime leaned his head back against the headboard and allowed himself to relax and surrender to the moment. It had been a long time since he had felt this safe with one of his johns. Usually he kept one eye on the door, in case the guy he was with decided to do something crazy. He could tell instinctively that Tim wasn't at all like that.

Steadily, Tim increased his pace, sweat forming on his brow and across his chest and dripping down onto Jaime, who began to rock his head back and forth. Tim gripped both of Jaime's legs firmly, continually running his hands from his calves to his ankles. The powerfully hypnotic pressure began to build to its crescendo, and Tim bucked onward as Jaime lifted his buttocks from the mattress to meet the force of impact. The sounds of the rapid-fire battery filled the small room, and Tim began to shout just as he ejaculated into the condom.

Tim cried out again before rolling onto his back. He looked over at Jaime, who smiled back at him.

"Wow, that was fucking fantastic," Tim said enthusiastically, reaching over and brushing Jaime's shaggy bangs from his face.

"It was also good for me. You want to pay me now and for me to leave?" Jaime asked. This was the standard method of operation of the men who paid for his services.

"How much would you charge me if you just stayed the night here?" Tim questioned.

"I do not know. No one has ever asked me to stay before," Jaime said, his eyes expressing bewilderment at the proposition.

"Not to worry. We'll figure it all out tomorrow morning. We can both get some sleep now," Tim replied, turning off the light.

⭐ 12

Tim awoke with the incessant cricketlike chirping of his cell phone ringing in his ears. He opened his eyes to see the bright light of day streaking through the window of the motel room. For a moment, he was disoriented and could not remember where he was. He had a dull headache and there was a foul taste in his mouth. Glancing over the bed, he saw Jaime stirring, and the memories of the night before came rushing back to him.

Naked, he stood up from the bed to retrieve the cell phone, buried deep within the front pocket of his trousers.

"Hello?" he managed to say groggily into the phone.

"Tim! Dear God! Where the hell are you?" The voice belonged to David, and the urgency in his tone caused Tim's heart to skip a few beats.

"David? Is that you?" Tim asked, placing a clammy hand to his forehead, which felt feverish to the touch.

"Who else would it be? Do you know how many calls I've fielded from producers, directors, and tabloid journalists, wondering where you are? Poor Ruth has been on the phone all night trying to locate you since you bolted from that rehab clinic. How many goddamn cell phones do you have, anyway? Eventually, I had to call the telephone company and pretend to be you to get the number. I even sent you an e-mail, hoping that you had your laptop with you."

The gravity of the situation began to clear his muddled mind. "Jeez, David, I'm sorry to have worried everybody. I just had to get away from that place and be by myself for a while, that's all. It certainly is good to hear your voice again, though," Tim added tenderly. It had been months since they had spoken.

"Dammit, Tim. Your life really has gotten off course lately and I'm concerned for your well-being. I didn't spend eleven years building up your career just to have you flush everything down the toilet," he scolded harshly.

"It makes me feel good to know that you still care, in spite of everything," Tim said softly. Jaime was now wide-awake and watching him from the bed.

"I will always care for you. You have to know that."

Tears stung Tim's eyes. "I guess I should know that, shouldn't I? Truth is, I'm not feeling too well at the moment."

"No kidding. You still haven't kicked your addiction to pain pills, my friend. You are probably going to go through a nasty withdrawal unless you get yourself back to the clinic."

"I don't think I can hack it at that clinic, David. Isn't there someplace closer to home I can go to, maybe on an outpatient basis?" Tim pleaded, the thought of returning to the Salvation Center in Palm Desert filling him with dread.

"There is a place here in Malibu. It's called Milagros, and plenty of actors and rock stars have been successful graduates. I'll make some calls to see what I can do. In the meantime, you had better call the studio to let them know you're okay. I just pray that they don't file a breach-of-contract lawsuit against you. They're already talking about doing some major rewrites on *A Mission from Hell* and possibly recasting the lead." David knew that this was not a time to mince his words. Tim was facing some serious troubles.

Tim groaned. "What happened to my life?" he asked, knowing perfectly well that he had no one else to blame but himself.

Suddenly, Jaime coughed loudly, the noise resonating in the confined space of the room. Tim tried to push the mute button, but it was too late.

David's voice changed from caring to professional when he spoke again. "I might have known that you wouldn't be alone, Tim. Just more of the same from you, I see. I have to go. Do yourself a favor and call the studio, then get back to LA from wherever in hell you are at right now. Good-bye, Tim. Call me when you get your act together." Then he angrily hung up the phone.

Tim cursed himself silently as he stared at the now-quiet telephone. His head had begun to pound more intensely, and he felt sick to his stomach.

"I'm sorry. Did I cause you any problems?" Jaime asked, standing up from the bed to put his clothes on.

"No. Don't worry about it. I've just got a bit of a situation on my hands, that's all. I suppose you'll be wanting your money now so you can be on your way." His head was killing him and he really needed to take something, anything, for the pain.

"*Sí*, that would be fine." Jaime was staring at Tim's nakedness as he stumbled around the room, trying to locate his pants that had been tossed beneath the bed in the mad dash to answer the phone. With any luck, he had a package of aspirin in the pockets.

Once Tim was back into his clothes, he had a moment of clarity. Jaime was sitting on the bed morosely, tracing the swirling pattern of the cheap bedspread with his finger, knowing that he had to go back out onto the streets again, where he would not have the relative comforts the cheap motel room had to offer. Tim watched his beautiful face, downcast with sadness. He couldn't just pay him a hundred bucks and then release him back to an uncertain future on the streets. Maybe there was a way he could help the boy.

"I was thinking," he said, finding a package of aspirin in his back trouser pocket. "I might be able to offer you a job or something. I mean, it would be better than living on the streets, wouldn't it?"

Jaime stared back at him, not knowing how to respond. "You are offering me a job?" he asked cautiously, unsure whether he had heard him correctly.

"Sure. I have a pretty big house with a pool and garden. It's hard to keep good help. But you would have to come back with me to Los Angeles where I live. Do you have family here in San Diego?"

Jaime shook his head. "No. I have nobody here," he responded.

"Good. I have to leave for LA right away. First I have to take something for this headache, and then we can be on our way."

Jaime smiled his first genuine smile in more than eight months. "*Bueno.* I promise I will do a good job for you."

"I'm sure you will," Tim said, popping the aspirin into his mouth and allowing the bitter pills to dissolve directly onto his tongue.

Tim was feeling a little better once they hit the freeway and were on their way to Los Angeles. The aspirin had helped to relieve the pounding of his headache, but his stomach was still in knots. Jaime had been hungry, so he pulled into the drive-through of a fast-food joint and ordered him an egg and sausage biscuit with cheese, which he quickly snarfed down. Tim had ordered one for himself but did not feel like eating it, so he gave the wrapped package to Jaime, who gratefully accepted it and gulped it down.

The two chatted amiably on the drive; Tim asked questions which Jaime answered shyly. He spoke very good English and, as far as Tim could tell, Jaime had not a clue as to who he was. Jaime admitted that he did not have the opportunity to watch very much television or to attend the movies while growing up in the small village in Guanajuato.

When Tim told him that he was a movie actor, Jaime's face lit up in surprise. "You act in the movies?" he asked in disbelief.

"Yes, I do. It was quite nice not having someone recognize me for a change. Sometimes, I forget what it's like to be a normal human being."

"You are a very lucky man. You have so many nice things and can provide for your family." Jaime's voice trailed off in sadness and regret.

Tim took note of his countenance and tone of voice. "Actually, I've never provided much for my family. They don't agree with how I live my life, and we have not spoken in many, many years."

Jaime looked back at him as if the concept of not being close to one's family was alien and unimaginable. "Family is very important. Sometimes, they are the only thing you have in this world," he said, his dark eyes no longer focusing on Tim but clouded with memories.

Tim could not think of an appropriate response. "We should make it to Los Angeles in good time," he said suddenly, changing the subject. "The traffic is moving smoothly and the weather is great. I think you will like it in LA."

Jaime looked back at Tim again, his face now brightened with a smile. "I'm sure that I will love it," he said, his mind filled with the prospect of a new life and the possibility of finding happiness and a respectable way to provide for his family back in Mexico.

Ruth Borstein stood beneath the imported Swarovski crystal chandelier in the foyer of Tim's Bel Air estate, tapping the heel of her kidskin pump furiously against the freshly waxed mosaic-tiled floor. Her thin arms were akimbo, and a look of consternation was deeply etched onto her face. She was wearing the vintage yellow and black Chanel suit that her departed husband Edgar had bought for her—as she was quick to tell anyone who would listen whenever she wore the outfit—at the Galeries Lafayette in Paris during a trip to Europe in 1958. She was most proud of the fact that the suit still fit her perfectly after all of these years.

"There you are, *meshugge!* I've practically pulled out all of my thinning gray hair worrying about you!" she exclaimed.

At the age of eighty-two, Ruth had not lost any of her spunkiness or zest for life. Although she had unofficially stepped down from most of her duties at the agency, her name remained on the company letterhead. She still drove herself from her house in Holmby Hills to the office in her gas-guzzling Cadillac at least three times a week, and she enjoyed chatting with clients and gossiping with the secretaries. She could not imagine going into full retirement; what purpose would there be to life?

Tim smiled at her, his face burning a bright red. He felt quite embarrassed and ashamed to have warranted a scolding from Ruth. "I'm sorry to have worried you and David," he said, flashing his megawatt smile at her in a blatant attempt to win her over.

Ruth's expression softened. "I'm just happy that you are alive and I won't be sitting shivah like a nice, old Jewish lady for the next few weeks."

She turned her attention to Jaime, who was standing behind Tim, admiring the palatial foyer. "And who might this handsome young man be?" she inquired, inspecting Jaime's appearance from top to bottom.

Tim spoke quickly. "Ruth, this is Jaime Adame. I've just hired him to do some odd jobs about the house and garden. You know how difficult it is to find good help these days."

From behind her tortoise-shell-framed glasses, Ruth narrowed her eyes knowingly at Tim. "Yes, I've heard," she said. "It's nice to meet you, Jaime."

Jaime accepted Ruth's extended hand to shake. "Nice to meet you," he echoed.

"Tim, it's time for some serious damage control. The studio has blown a gasket after this latest stunt of yours, I'm afraid. They are seriously considering recasting the lead with one of those aging action-hero stars. There's also talk of bringing in a big name costar, that is if they allow you to return to the film at all. David, bless his heart, has been on a nonstop conference call since the shit hit the fan yesterday. That man still loves you deeply, you know," Ruth remarked, ever hopeful that there would be a reconciliation between the two.

Tim sighed and lowered his head. "I know, Ruth. I'm afraid I've really fucked things up royally this time. Do you think I can recover from this mess?"

"Of course you can, sweetie. This is just a small bump in the road compared to some of the scandals people in this town have starred in. The first course of action will be to get you back into rehab somewhere. The studio won't budge on that demand. As soon as they hand you a clean bill of health and your piss runs as pure as a Colorado mountain spring, they will allow you to return to the set. But no more monkey business. You are not in a position to act like a diva now. Whatever the bosses say, goes. Understood?"

Tim nodded in agreement. "Understood. David said he would try to get me into some New Age rehab center out in Malibu. At least if I'm there, you guys will keep a watchful eye on me so I won't be tempted to slip up. I swear to you, there will be no more drugs in my life, with God as my witness," he said, raising his right hand to the sky with his left hand over his heart.

"I will be holding you to that promise," Ruth declared, smiling at him lovingly. She and Edgar had never had any children, and Tim was practically a grandson to her.

"Has anyone heard from Raina?" Tim asked, knowing that she too was probably frantic with worry.

"She's only called about a thousand times. I was surprised that even she did not have access to your top-secret cell phone number, the way you two live in each other's pockets. You had better call her back and notify her that you are among the living," Ruth advised.

Jaime was shifting his weight back and forth from his left to right foot out of boredom. Tim turned to him. "Jaime, I'd better show you to your quarters. After I've straightened out the disaster I've made of my life, I'll find something for you to do."

Ruth pursed her lips and glanced over at the young man before looking at Tim disapprovingly. "I'm certain you already have some duties in mind for him, don't you, my dear?"

"This will be your room," Tim said, opening the door to the bedroom just down the hall from Tim's master suite on the upper level of the house. The decor of the room was French Provincial, and a balcony overlooked the Olympic-size swimming pool and the lush, landscaped gardens. This was only the third or fourth time Tim had even entered the room; the Mediterranean-style house had a total of fifteen bedrooms and twelve and a half baths.

Jaime's mouth was agape as he looked around the room. "I will be sleeping here?" he asked in astonishment.

"If the room is to your liking," Tim replied.

"This room is bigger than the entire house I grew up in," Jaime said without exaggeration.

Tim laughed softly. "Well, you don't have to sleep here every night, of course," he whispered in a conspiratorial fashion. "My bedroom is just down the hall," he added with a wink.

Jaime smiled with his mouth closed, which accentuated the deep dimples in his cheeks. He cast his gaze down to the floor again. He was unaccustomed to people being so kind to him in this country.

"Well, I'll leave you to get settled in," Tim said. He knew that Jaime had brought with him only a threadbare knapsack containing all of his worldly possessions, but there was much for Tim to do. First on the list was to call Raina to let her know that he was alive and well.

"Thank you again, Tim. For bringing me here with you and for letting me stay in your beautiful house."

"No problem, Jaime," Tim replied, resisting the temptation to caress the high cheekbones of his striking face. "I will see you later. Feel free to walk around and explore the house and outside gardens. Make yourself at home."

He paused for a brief second at the door and watched Jaime's exuberance at being in the luxurious surroundings of the room, a place where he could feel safe and protected for the first time in many, many months. He then closed the door and allowed Jaime to enjoy his reverie in private.

"Thank heavens, Tim," Raina said with relief in her voice. "I've been so concerned about you. I didn't sleep a wink last night and I've had newspapers and television shows calling the house nonstop. I must have said the words 'no comment' a million times."

"I'm sorry, Raina. I should have called you right away. I didn't realize that leaving rehab would create such a firestorm of controversy," Tim said, looking into his own bloodshot eyes in the bathroom mirror as he spoke into the telephone. He truly looked as if he had gone a couple of rounds with a prizefighter. His head was beginning to pound again and he felt drained of all energy. He fumbled in the medicine cabinet for some eyedrops.

"Sometimes you forget that you are a superstar," Raina chided. She neglected to mention that she too often forgot she was famous and was startled when strangers called out her name in public. "Why don't you come over to my new house? You've never even been inside my home," she said in her petulant, little-girl voice. Raina had recently purchased an 11,000-square-foot English country-style mansion, complete with an ivy-covered facade, in the newly chic enclave of Hancock Park, close to the grounds of the exclusive Wilshire Country

Club. "What's the purpose of spending all of that money on the house when no one even comes to visit me?"

"I promise to come over and visit you once all of this nonsense blows over. I only hope I haven't been fired from *A Mission from Hell*. I've been fired before and, as I recall, it really bites."

"There was something I was going to discuss with you. Oh, yeah. David called me this morning and was grilling me about you and whether you were seeing someone new. He seems to be under the impression that you were with someone last night." Raina paused for effect. "So, who's the lucky guy? Anyone I know?"

"Trust me, it wouldn't be anyone you know. He's about as far from the Hollywood type as one can get. How did David sound when he spoke with you?" Tim asked, curious about David's mood after their conversation that morning.

"You know David. He's still very possessive of you. But who could blame him? You're such a heartbreaker," Raina said playfully. "I hope I get to meet this mystery man soon."

"Maybe. Things are kind of chaotic now," Tim remarked noncommittally. "I still have to endure another stint in boot camp to appease the studio and prove that I'm clean and sober."

"This is all so very *Valley of the Dolls*. Hey, I was just reading in the papers about this Dr. Feelgood who has a clinic on the Caribbean island of St. Kitts. He swears he can get anyone off any type of drug using a treatment derived from an African root. Of course, the drug is illegal here in the States as it's a hallucinogenic, but the clinic is a quick plane ride away," Raina offered helpfully.

"I don't think I'm that far gone, sweetie pie. Besides, David told me he could pull a few strings and get me admitted to Milagros out in Malibu."

Raina harrumphed. "David knows best, of course," she said, the familiar pout now in her voice. "What would I know about such things? After all, I'm just your simple-minded yet loyal fag hag."

"Now don't be that way, my love. I promise that I will talk to you soon. I have yet to phone the studio, and I'm sure they're calling for my head on a platter. Don't worry about me. I am going to be fine," Tim said.

"I have every faith that you will," Raina replied. "Take care, my dear. I fully expect to have a detailed report about your love life the next time we speak."

"Duly noted. Kisses."

"Kisses," Raina echoed before disconnecting.

★ 14

The photographer had no trouble scaling the tall and leafy California oak and finding the perfect spot to peer over the twelve-foot-high security fence and spy on the estate grounds. He had been doing this sort of thing for the past several decades and was an old pro at scouting out the ideal location for taking photographs of people who did not wish to be photographed. With his trusty, forty-year-old Nikon camera hanging from a leather strap around his neck, he looked out from his perch several houses down from Tim Race's mansion on Stone Canyon Road, less than a mile from the fabled Hotel Bel-Air. Many newbies had trouble navigating the confusing, pretzel-shaped roads of the neighborhood, but he kept a map of the area fresh in his mind. He had encountered a handful of other photographers that morning, acquaintances that he knew on a first-name basis, but they were hanging out near the front gate to the house. That was far too easy for him; he liked a challenge.

Many of his pictures had landed on the front covers of various supermarket tabloids over the years. He earned a yearly six-figure-plus income from his endeavors. Naturally, inherent risks were involved in celebrity photography: temperamental stars going on a rampage, overzealous bodyguards, vicious attack dogs, and, of course, falling out of trees.

This assignment appeared to be a relatively easy one; all he had to do was snap a picture of Tim Race somewhere outside of his home. He didn't have to be doing anything special; he could be doing something mundane like picking up the morning paper or drinking coffee by the pool. After the news broke that Tim had gone AWOL from the Salvation Drug and Alcohol Treatment Center, the price for his snapshot had suddenly skyrocketed. One of the tabloids he regularly contributed photographs to had contacted him earlier that morning with the scoop on Tim Race. He had photographed Tim several times before, mostly on the red carpet outside of movie premieres, hanging on the arm of the ravishing Raina Hawthorne. They were an extremely photogenic pair, and a picture of the two together, dressed to the nines, was always a moneymaker.

As the photographer surveyed the area by the swimming pool from his vantage point high in the tree, he noticed movement. Looking through the camera lens, he focused on a figure now standing beneath the faux-Corinthian columns that formed the entryway to the pool.

Jaime had somehow managed to find his way outside of the immense house and to the swimming pool. Tim's home was a confusing labyrinth of passageways and massive rooms; at least, it was confusing to Jaime. The sun was burning hotly overhead as he walked down the tiled steps to the pool, sweat quickly forming on his brow.

He sat down on a damask-covered chaise longue beside the bubbling Jacuzzi. A large-screen television protected behind waterproof glass sat directly in front of the Jacuzzi, which seated up to eight people. Jaime removed his tennis shoes and stared out at the enticing water of the swimming pool. He looked back toward the main house but did not see anyone. He had not seen Tim since earlier that afternoon. He had become bored and restless waiting in the bedroom, so he took it upon himself to explore the house and grounds.

Finally, Jaime decided to take the plunge. He pulled his T-shirt over his head and dropped his pants. Unfettered from his clothing, he gave one last look toward the house before diving headfirst into the pool. The cool, refreshing water instantly encased his naked body in a calming cocoon. He swam to the opposite end of the pool and turned back. He playfully skirted the bottom of the pool, doing graceful underwater somersaults before surfacing to take a breath. He laughed out loud once he had surfaced, feeling as carefree and happy as any eighteen-year-old swimming in the lap of luxury should. Jaime paddled back to the bottom of the pool once again, his nude body slicing its way through the clear water.

When he surfaced for the second time, he noticed a figure bathed in shadows standing at the far end of the pool.

"I see you are already beginning to enjoy the comforts around here," Tim shouted.

Jaime smiled and laughed, treading water before taking a drink into his mouth and spewing it out like a stream from an ancient Roman fountain. "You want to swim with me?" he asked playfully, doing a backstroke, his flaccid penis resting against his tanned leg just above the waterline.

Tim could feel his hard-on straining against the cloth of his pants. "I wish I could. Unfortunately, I have some more business to take care of. My bosses want to meet with me at the studio. It looks like you're going to be quite fine here. Enjoy the pool for as long as you want. If you get hungry, you can go into the kitchen, which is right through those doors over there," Tim said, pointing toward the house.

Jaime was now at the pool ladder. He climbed out of the water, beads of liquid shimmering on his body in the golden light of the late afternoon sun. Tim admired the deliciously youthful body again as he handed him a bright yellow terry-cloth towel to dry himself. Jaime's dimpled smile tugged at Tim's heartstrings.

"Gracias," he said as he dried his hair with the towel. He sat on the chaise longue and languorously toweled off his body before putting his clothes back on. Tim watched silently from his standing position.

Tim's voice was low and husky when he spoke. "If you would like, we can have dinner together tonight in the dining hall. I'll have my cook Mariana prepare us something Mexican."

"Thank you," Jaime said, draping the towel around his neck. "I am a little hungry now."

"Good. I will be gone for only a short while. You know the way back to the house. I'll see you later tonight."

Jaime got up from the chaise and stood in front of Tim, toe to toe, before pulling him into his arms for a warm and appreciative hug. "Thank you again, for all of this," he whispered into his ear.

Tim hugged him in return, patting him affectionately on the back. His still-damp body felt wonderfully comfortable in his arms, as if he belonged there all along. Tim broke the embrace abruptly. "Goodbye, Jaime. I'll see you soon," he said quickly, turning on his heels to leave.

"Adíos," Jaime replied, but Tim had already bounded up the stairs to the house and had dashed out of view.

From the oak tree several hundred yards away, the photographer placed the cap back on the lens to his camera and smiled in satisfaction. The pictures he had taken would certainly bring him a pretty penny. It would probably earn him more than enough money to take the wife and kids on a wonderful family vacation to Disney World in Florida. They would stay in the nicest hotel in the park and eat at the most expensive restaurants, renting a luxury SUV to take them wherever their hearts desired. *All in all, life as a shutterbug is damn good,* he thought to himself cheerfully as he climbed down the tree and ambled undetected along the peaceful avenue.

Jaime ate dinner in the massive dining room, alone. Mariana, Tim's cook, had prepared him a plateful of delicious cheese quesadillas smothered in homemade red mole sauce that she had spent the entire previous day making. She chatted with him in her animated style while she cooked the food in the ultramodern kitchen. She was from the state of Michoacan, where most of her family remained. She asked if Jaime was gay, which caught him a little off guard. He blushed brightly, but Mariana just laughed, telling him not to worry. Having worked for Mr. Race for two and a half years, she pretty much knew what was what around the house. She told him about Tim's longtime "friend," David, and how they recently had had a nasty breakup. Jaime listened intently as she prepared the meal.

An hour later, after Tim had failed to appear, Jaime entered the dining hall with the large Chippendale table and ate his meal of quesadillas in silence. The house was indeed too quiet for his liking; he was accustomed to the cacophony of noise that a large family produced. The food was particularly appetizing; it had been so long since he had eaten a home-cooked meal.

Feeling restless, he prowled the house again, exploring the many rooms and endless corridors. He practically had to pinch himself every few minutes; this all seemed like an incredible dream. He came upon the media room, which housed every possible technological entertainment device that existed on the earth. There were pinball machines and arcade video games, jukeboxes, DVD players, computers, stereos, and large-screen televisions. He felt as if he were window shopping at a luxury department store.

Passing through a set of swinging doors with porthole windows and crushed, red velvet padding, he found himself standing in an actual movie theater! There were rows of seats and an enormous screen partially hidden behind a large, red velvet curtain. There was even a popcorn machine and soda fountain along with a long glass case full of boxed candies and bags of potato chips. Jaime could not believe his eyes. He simply could not imagine that people actually lived this way.

He sat down on one of the comfortable theater chairs and propped his feet up on the back of the seat in front of him. Sitting in the darkened theater, he imagined himself back in Mexico, attending with his brothers and sisters an old Western movie starring the Mexican matinee idol Vicente Fernandez, his mother and father watching lovingly over them all. The thought made Jaime sigh, and he leaned his head back and closed his eyes. Within moments, he was fast asleep.

Tim looked nervously at his Patek Phillipe Calatrava gold watch for the fifth time in as many minutes. He still didn't feel up to par, and he really wanted out of the stark conference room where the impromptu meeting had been called. The president of the studio, John Whitmore, was seated at the head of the table, a dour look on his face. Around him sat a roomful of accountants, publicists, and other members of the studio board, all wearing the same dismal expression.

Mr. Whitmore spoke in a deep, authoritative voice. "Now, Tim, we here at the studio are immensely aware of your tremendous contribution to our financial success. But your most recent behavior has left us in a bit of a quandary. As you are fully aware, the studio has invested a considerable amount of money in *A Mission from Hell*. You are also aware that your continued participation in the film is contingent on your seeking help for a substance abuse problem. We have been perfectly willing to pay for your enrollment in such a program, but you have seen fit to leave rehabilitation without so much as telling anyone. As you can imagine, that puts me in a rather awkward position." He paused to take a drink of water and looked at Tim expectantly.

Tim felt like a schoolboy being admonished by the headmaster. "I'm aware that I've caused an inconvenience to you and to the studio, Mr. Whitmore. I profusely apologize for my behavior, for which there is no excuse. I give you my solemn oath that I will seek professional help for my problem and that I will not cause any more delays in the production of *A Mission from Hell.*"

A thin smile touched Mr. Whitmore's lips. "I'm happy to hear that, Tim. However, we feel that some other measures are needed to ensure that the film is completed to the studio's satisfaction. The writers of the film's script have agreed to do some rewrites and to add another character, to alleviate some of the pressure on you to make the film a success. We've contacted Frederick van Nostrand and he's agreed to join the film's production."

Tim tried not to allow his dismay show on his face. Frederick van Nostrand was an aging European action hero. He was a lousy actor who could hardly speak English, but he was a master in martial arts and still had a terrific body. His films also brought in truckloads of money. Tim could not believe that the studio actually had the gall to hire a big-name costar for one of his films.

Remembering Ruth's warning not to act like a diva, Tim swallowed his opinions before speaking. "If that's what you believe is necessary to complete the movie, then I do not have a problem with it, sir."

"I'm glad that to hear that, Tim. I expect you to enroll in a substance abuse program locally within the next few days. I also expect you to report to duty on time when filming is rescheduled." He stood up to leave. "As always, it's good to speak with you, Tim."

Tim rose and shook Mr. Whitmore's hand. "A pleasure, sir. I promise you that I won't let you down."

"Wonderful. If you should have any problems, don't hesitate to contact me here at the office. You are one of our favorite stars around here, Tim. I hope you stay that way," he added as he left the conference room, his retinue of hangers-on following suit.

Tim sat down in the chair again once the room had cleared. He put his head in his hands and sighed. "I'm screwed," he said to himself.

★ 15

Jaime opened his eyes and immediately jolted up from the chair. It was a reflexive action, for he had grown used to waking up in dangerous surroundings, ready to take flight at a second's notice. It took a moment for him to realize that he was not in any danger and that he had fallen asleep in the movie theater of Tim's mansion. He stood up and stretched before strolling out of the theater. Once in the light, he looked at the digital watch he had lifted off one of his more unpleasant johns while he was asleep. It couldn't be seven o'clock in the morning! Jaime tried to remember the path he had taken to reach the theater. After a few minutes, he found his way back to the kitchen, where Mariana was already preparing breakfast.

"*Dios mio!*" she exclaimed, examining his rough appearance. "Where did you sleep last night? It could not have been in Mr. Race's bed."

Jaime grinned at her. "No, *tonta*. I fell asleep in the movie theater. Have you seen that place? It's incredible."

"The only part of Mr. Race's house that I get to see is the kitchen and dining room, and that's fine with me," she replied, mixing pancake batter in a glass bowl.

"Did Tim, I mean Mr. Race, come home last night?" Jaime asked, wondering if he had been missed.

"*Sí.* He's already awake and in the dining room," Mariana said, pointing in the direction of the dining hall.

Jaime excused himself and entered the dining room. Tim was reading the morning newspaper and drinking a cup of coffee. He looked up when Jaime entered the room, an expression of pleasant surprise on his face.

"There you are, Jaime! I thought that you had taken off without telling me good-bye. I was very worried when I checked your room last night and didn't find you there. I looked all over the house and the grounds and couldn't find you. Where on earth did you sleep last night?" Tim's voice reflected his concern, but also relief that Jaime had not run away.

"I am sorry that I worried you. I was, how do you say, *exploring* the house. I found the theater. It's such an amazing place. I guess I fell asleep and did not wake up until this morning."

Tim laughed and took a sip of his coffee. "That theater is neat, isn't it? It's my favorite part of the house too. It's actually the reason I bought the house. Please, sit down and have some breakfast. I hope that Mariana made you something wonderful to eat last night."

"Oh, yes. She is a very good cook," Jaime said as he sat down in the chair opposite Tim. "How did things go with your meeting last night?"

"Not very well, I'm afraid," Tim said. "It seems that I've made my bosses very angry. I don't want to bore you with the details." He reached over and brushed Jaime's bangs from his forehead. "You really could use a haircut. I also imagine you need some new clothes. Tell you what. I've got some business to tend to in the city today. Why don't you come with me and I can take you to the salon and to buy some new clothes."

Jaime smiled excitedly. "That would be nice. I have been wearing these clothes for a long time," he said, looking down at his T-shirt and jeans, which had been his uniform for over eight months. "I do not have the money to pay for these things now, but I promise I will work very hard for you to pay you back."

"Don't worry about it. I brought you all the way here from San Diego; the least I could do is buy you some nice clothes and pay for a haircut."

Later that morning, Tim drove Jaime to the Christophe Hair Salon on North Beverly Drive. It was where he always went to have his hair trimmed and styled, and he knew the staff quite well and was certain that they could be trusted. Jaime had no idea how he wanted to have his hair styled, but the pretty, effeminate male hairstylist with the adorable Irish accent raved about the thickness and color of Jaime's hair. He cut several inches off the top and sides, shearing the hair in the back very short with the clippers. He then trimmed his long, shaggy bangs. When finished, he spiked up Jaime's new 'do with a sandalwood-scented pomade. Jaime looked at himself in the mirror, scarcely recognizing the person staring back at him. Tim tipped the hairstylist a fifty before escorting Jaime out of the salon.

They then headed to the Neiman Marcus department store on Wilshire Boulevard, where Tim used the valet parking entrance. He tipped the cute, buff parking attendant twenty dollars before rushing into the department store, Jaime following in quick pursuit. They immediately hit the men's clothing department, where a lovely female member of the personable but not oversolicitous staff served them. Tim quickly snapped up several cashmere polo sweaters, Hugo Boss jeans, Izod shirts, and a pair of size ten Prada sneakers for Jaime. The smiling female clerk did not ask any questions when Tim produced his credit card to pay for the expensive items.

Before leaving, they stopped at the eyewear department, where Tim bought two pairs of matching Oakley Straight Jacket polarized sunglasses, one for Jaime and the other for himself. As they left the store, weighed down with bags, Tim's cell phone rang. With his arms full, he struggled to answer the phone.

"Where are you, my love?" Raina asked cheerfully.

"Neiman Marcus, doing a little shopping," Tim replied.

"Splendid. I just had a manicure and pedicure at Ripsy's and now I'm quite hungry. Why don't you and I meet somewhere for an early lunch?"

"Sounds great," Tim said as the valet brought his Mercedes around. He handed the stud another twenty-dollar bill. "Where should we meet up?"

"How about Mauro's Cafe?" Raina replied.

"Perfect. Just so you'll know, I have company with me."

"Really? I'm intrigued. I'll see you in about ten minutes."

Precisely ten minutes later, Raina roared up to the Italian bistro on trendy Melrose Avenue in her canary yellow Porsche Boxster. Wearing an umber-toned peasant blouse, faded hip-huggers, cork-soled wedgies, and minimal makeup, she looked the vision of hippie chic. She lifted up her sunglasses and arched her recently waxed eyebrows as she approached the outdoor table where Tim sat with Jaime.

"Hey there, beautiful," she said, bending down to give Tim a kiss on his cheek. "It feels like it's been forever since we've seen each other." She licked her thumb and gently brushed away the coral lipstick smudge she had left on Tim's cheek.

"I know, I'm sorry. Things have just been so nuts with me lately, as you are fully aware," Tim replied apologetically.

"Actually, there appear to be quite a few things that I don't know about your life these days. You haven't introduced me to your *young* friend here yet," Raina said, looking directly at Jaime.

"This is Jaime. He works for me now," Tim said. "We were just out shopping for some things he needs for his new job."

"Oh," Raina responded. "And just what is your new job?" she asked Jaime, who was avoiding eye contact with her.

"He's now taking care of my garden and pool," Tim answered for Jaime.

"Really? He doesn't even appear to be of legal working age. Or is he legal *period?*"

"Excuse me," Jaime interrupted, desperate to get away from the unfolding melodrama. "I need to go to the bathroom."

Tim pointed inside the restaurant. "It's inside and to your right," he directed.

Raina waited until Jaime was out of hearing range. "Have you lost your mind? What are you thinking, bringing some illegal Mexican jailbait out in public and parading him around the city where you could be photographed? And don't tell me you are doing research for an upcoming episode of *Queer As Folk* either. Is this the guy that you spent the other night with?" she demanded reprovingly.

"Raina, calm down. I'm in no mood to be judged or criticized. It's been a horrible past few weeks and I don't feel like explaining myself. The studio is riding my ass hard and they just brought in Frederick van Nostrand to costar in the movie. I've got to enter a treatment center or else I'm fired and my career will be in the dumper. David is still furious with me. Not to mention I feel like death warmed over. So I needed a little diversion to take my mind off things. What's the harm?"

Raina sighed in exasperation and covered her eyes with her hand. "What's the harm, you ask? The last thing you need is another scandal to blow up in your face. That would make the studio so very happy with you. And you are complaining about David being furious with you, but from where I stand, he has every reason to be upset. I just don't understand what is going on with you lately. Are you going through some early midlife crisis or something?" she asked.

"Oh, Raina, I don't know. I feel like I'm drowning and nobody will throw me a life jacket. It all started when I won that goddamn Academy Award. My life has been spiraling out of control ever since."

"I don't think you can put the blame for what is going on in your life on Mr. Oscar. I am really worried about you. And now with you and this underage boy . . ."

"For your information, Jaime is eighteen years old, so he is of legal age," Tim retorted.

"Thank heaven for small miracles. Look, I know that I don't have the right to judge you, but I am your best friend, so I would be remiss in my obligations if I didn't at least express my concerns to you. I'm afraid that the path you are traveling is going to lead you to nothing but pain and misery. I don't want to see you going through that. I care far too much about you," she said tenderly, reaching across the table and touching his face.

Tim took her hand and kissed it lovingly. "I know that you care and I love you for it. You are the best friend that I have ever had in my entire life," he said truthfully, for he had never connected to another human being the way he connected with Raina.

When Jaime returned to the table, Raina pulled her hand gently from Tim's grasp. "Jaime, it was very nice to meet you. I just remembered that I have another appointment that completely slipped my mind. You two have a nice lunch without me. Tim, call me soon, okay?" she said, abruptly standing up. She bent to kiss Tim again on his cheek. "Please, be careful and think about what you are doing," she whispered in his ear before bolting off, the scent of patchouli trailing after her.

"Your friends don't like me very much, do they?" Jaime asked sadly as Tim watched Raina take off in the Porsche Boxster.

"They are just a little confused, that's all. They don't understand what's going on," Tim replied.

"I don't think I understand what is going on either," Jaime muttered under his breath.

★ 16

The Milagros Rehabilitation Center was located in a former private residence on a promontory in Malibu, overlooking the ocean to the west and a fire-swept canyon to the east. Its clientele of mainly wealthy and famous patients, who doled out close to $40,000 for a thirty-day stay, were often surprised by how spartan the clinic was. The dormitory-style rooms were all identical; each contained two beds with white covers, and the rooms were all painted the same dull, off-white color. All patients shared a communal bathroom and ate their bland meals in shifts in the monochromatic cafeteria.

After dropping Jaime off at the house, he had received an urgent voice mail from David instructing him to report to Milagros immediately. David had managed to pull some strings and arrange for Tim to receive treatment from the clinic on an outpatient basis. The clinic was very regimented and did not usually allow members to join as outpatients, but David had somehow managed, in his inimitable style, to persuade the staff to make an exception for him. Tim maneuvered his car carefully along the winding road leading to the clinic, which was often closed during rainy days due to the threat of mudslides. He dreaded having to go through treatment again, but he knew that it was a necessity if he wanted to start work on the movie.

Pulling up to the clinic entrance, he spotted David's candy-apple red Mustang parked out front. He caught his breath and could feel his heart beat faster in his chest. It thrilled him that he was there, but he realized that David would probably be stoic and indifferent with him, at least in front of the staff.

A nurse in uniform greeted him at the entrance. "Hello, Mr. Race. We've been expecting you. I'm Nurse Robertson and I will help check you into the treatment center and show you around Milagros. You have your first counseling session scheduled for this afternoon."

"Thank you," he replied. "Is Mr. Reardon inside?" he queried as they walked up the stairwell to the clinic's lobby.

"Yes, Mr. Reardon is inside, speaking with our director of admissions, Dr. Westhall. We understand that your case is difficult from most of our other cases here at the clinic, and we will do everything in our power to make your stay here as comfortable and constructive as possible."

Entering the lobby, Tim saw David speaking with a bald-headed gentleman wearing glasses and a white doctor's coat. David watched Tim as he approached, walking behind the nurse.

"Dr. Westhall, this is Mr. Race," the nurse said in introduction.

"Mr. Race. Very nice to meet you." The doctor spoke in a loud voice, shaking Tim's hand vigorously. "Mr. Reardon and I were just going over the specifics of your case. I hope that is all right."

Tim smiled back at the doctor. "Yes, that's perfectly fine. David has been my agent and PR person for years now. He's always had my best interests at heart," he said, staring into David's eyes, which momentarily harbored a look of caring before David broke the gaze.

"They have agreed to treat you on an outpatient basis, Tim. However, you must adhere to strict guidelines in order to remain in the program, per the studio's request," David said firmly, looking to Dr. Westhall for affirmation.

"That is correct, Mr. Race. We have a variety of different treatment programs for a host of addictions here at Milagros. It is paramount that you attend a one-hour counseling session with your therapist each day. You must submit to a mandatory drug screening weekly. And we ask that you do at least two hours of volunteer work a week here at the center. Nothing too menial, you understand, just some light cleaning or perhaps helping in the kitchen. The key to breaking any addiction is to form a healthy routine and to have continuous support and positive reinforcement from friends, other patients, and the staff. Vicodin addiction is a particularly strong one, Mr. Race, but we have treated thousands of patients for it and there is a negligible recidivism rate. Our program is one of the most successful drug treatments in the world."

"I'm happy to hear that," Tim responded, adding a cheerful note to his voice. "When is my first counseling session?"

"We can begin now, if you're ready. Dr. Janson will be your counselor for the duration of your treatment."

"Thank you, Dr. Westhall. Do you think that it would be possible to have a brief moment to consult with Mr. Reardon before my session begins?" Tim inquired.

"Of course. When you are done, Dr. Janson's office is down that hall, the first door on the right. Again, it was nice meeting you. I know that your time here will be highly productive." The doctor shook Tim's hand again before walking down the hall.

Tim turned to David. "Thank you, David. I know that you went above and beyond the call of duty in having me admitted here. You really saved my ass," he said sincerely.

"Don't mention it, Tim. I wasn't about to let you fall flat on your face. I still care about *your* health and happiness," David said, an unavoidable bitterness creeping into his voice.

Tim winced at the sound of his hurt. "I've really messed things up, David. Not just with my career and my life, but with you most of all. I guess I'm just hoping that we can at least come out of all this as friends."

"Friends? I used to be one of your best friends as well as your lover, confidant, and loyal supporter. But I guess that wasn't enough for you. Maybe no one is enough for you, Tim. Maybe you just can't be faithful out of fear of missing out on something in life. Who knows, that might be why you turned to drugs. That's for the shrinks to figure out, I suppose. I only know that I loved you more than anyone on this earth. I thought the feeling was mutual, but I was mistaken. You only have enough heart to love yourself, Tim. Fame is what feeds your damn ambition and ego. I only hope that your fame and fortune can love you the way I did," David said before turning away.

Tim couldn't find his breath to respond. He watched silently as David walked away and left the sterile environment of the clinic behind. Finding himself alone in the corridor, he leaned against the wall and wept like a child.

★ 17

Jaime switched the large-screen television to the Spanish-language network. The news was on, but nothing of interest to him was being reported. Sitting alone in the gigantic, lavish bedroom, he was beginning to wonder if he had made a wise decision in coming to Los Angeles with Tim. Things were starting to become complicated, especially with Tim's friends, who obviously did not approve of their relationship. But what was their relationship, exactly? They had had sex once, an act that Tim had paid for. Jaime knew for certain that if he stayed for very long in the house, he would fall in love with Tim. How could he not? Tim was an incredibly handsome man, with money and power and a beautiful home. He was also a fantastic lover. The memory of the sexual encounter the two had shared stirred a sudden longing within him. Tim was everything someone like Jaime could hope for in this world. Yet he knew that the very idea of the two of them as a couple was ridiculous. How could such a relationship ever work?

He was growing bored and restless. At least on the street he was never bored; he was always too busy looking over his shoulder for danger to be bored. Tim had promised him a job, but they had not discussed the issue further because Tim was always gone. He decided that it would be necessary to have a discussion with Tim, to find out what his place in this incredible new world would be. If there was no place for him, then he would have to leave and be on his own once again, as terrifying as that thought was to him.

"I'm sorry about my little episode earlier this afternoon," Raina said, binoculars in hand. She was spying from her bedroom window on the grounds of the adjacent Wilshire Country Club. She spotted Jack Nicholson on the greens with his entourage, playing through to the eighteenth hole. "You really caught me by surprise, Tim. I apologize for the way I acted. Jaime must think I'm some kind of horrible bitch."

Tim took the binoculars from her hand and surveyed the golf course. "I don't think he knew what to think about you, my dear," he teased, feeling lighthearted for the first time since speaking with David. "Darn. I don't see Kevin Costner anywhere."

Raina snatched the binoculars away from him. "Hey, this is my bedroom and I get to do all the covert spying."

Raina's bedroom was a feminine confectionery of pale pink and pastel colors. The furnishings were youthful yet elegant, which exactly suited her outgoing personality. It was the perfect room for a college-bound teenaged girl with great taste, if she happened to be worth $20 million.

"I was only trying to take my mind off what David said." Tim's tone had turned more serious. "He told me I wasn't truly capable of loving someone, that I could only love myself. Do you think that's true?"

"David is just hurt and trying to lash out at you. He didn't really mean what he said. You are a very loving person," Raina said, blowing him a kiss, which Tim pretended to catch in the palm of his hand.

After dusk fell, they both went downstairs to the grandiose den. On the wall above the pink marble fireplace hung the framed *Cosmopolitan* with Raina on the cover, the beautiful portrait taken by famed photographer Francesco Scavullo. They sat on her sofa in the warm and inviting den and ate from bags of microwave popcorn, Raina's favorite treat. They caught an old rerun of *Ain't That a Shame?* in syndication on cable and laughed hysterically at Raina's teased, big hair and trashy outfits.

"I should be heading back home," Tim said once all the popcorn had been consumed.

"You don't have to leave, you know," Raina replied. *"Mi casa es tu casa."*

"I know. I should really go home, though. It's time to square things away with Jaime."

Raina bolstered him with a resplendent smile. "Good luck, my love."

Tim found Jaime watching television in his bedroom. He stood up from the bed when Tim entered the room. "I'm so glad you are home."

"Jaime, I wanted to tell you that I'm sorry about the way things have been the past few days. I know that I brought you here from San Diego with the intention of helping you in some way. Things are a little crazy with my life right now, as you can probably see. I haven't been fair with you and I'm sorry."

"You don't have to say you are sorry to me. I am thankful that you have been so nice to me. I am not used to people being so nice to me. You saved my life."

Tim reached out to touch his face, stroking his newly trimmed hair, which made him look even more devastatingly handsome. "You are so beautiful," he whispered, the sting of David's words still fresh in his mind. David was wrong; he had to be wrong. He knew in his heart that he had loved David, that he still loved him, and that he was capable of loving again.

"I'm not sure I should stay here," Jaime said. "I make trouble with your friends. You are famous and people will talk. It would be best if I leave."

"But I don't want you to leave," Tim responded, feeling a small tickle of fear near the top of his rib cage. Tim knew the fear well; it was the fear of being abandoned, of being left alone and loveless in a cruel and hateful world.

"It is for the best, I believe. It is time for me to go back home to Mexico. My mama is there and she needs my help to take care of my brothers and sisters."

"I can help your mother. I can send her money, perhaps even bring her here to the States with your brothers and sisters." Tim heard the sudden desperation in his voice and took a deep breath to cover it. "Wouldn't you want to have your mother safe here in this country?" he asked.

"You would do that for me?" Jaime's eyes were now wet with tears.

"Of course I would. I would help you in any way I can."

"Oh, thank you," Jaime said, falling into Tim's arms. "I would do anything to help my family."

Tim lifted Jaime's chin with his fist and stared deeply into his dark, soulful eyes. "It would make me happy to do something good for someone else, for a change." Tim's eyes looked away from Jaime's gaze for a brief moment before settling on him once again. He smiled, the faintest of creases forming around his eyelids and near the corners of his mouth.

"I don't know how to repay you, Tim." Jaime moved his lips closer to Tim's.

"You'll think of a way," Tim said softly as he bent his face forward to kiss Jaime, parting his soft lips and seeking out the warmth of his tongue. Jaime moaned, dropping his hands to the buttons on Tim's shirt. With expert hands, he unbuttoned his shirt, nuzzling Tim's neck and seeking out the chiseled hardness of his pectorals. His tongue found the rigid peaks that had formed on each flinching muscle, drawing them one by one into his mouth for a brief moment of pleasure. Tim ran his fingers through Jaime's freshly shorn hair before helping him out of his brand-new polo shirt. Once free from their clothing, they moved to the bed and fell onto the soft nest of covers and pillows. They kissed again, a long, slow, passionate kiss, their eyes closed as each explored the other's mouth, making mental maps of the sweet, delicious cavity.

Jaime was the first to pull away. Staring into Tim's eyes, he shifted his weight, then bowed his head toward his groin. He held Tim's cock in his hand, methodically massaging the head and monitoring the expressions on his face. With a practiced ease, Jaime drew him into his mouth and immediately began rotating his tongue in rapid circles around the head. He dragged his tongue adroitly around the swollen crown of Tim's cock, causing him to toss his head sharply from left to right, his breath coming in quick, shallow pants. Tim cupped the sides of Jaime's face in his hands, watching in thrilled fascination as he found his rhythm, engulfing the entire length of him with his mouth.

Tim felt the exquisite pressure building up from the power source he wielded between his legs. Jaime stared up at him, measuring the quickness of Tim's breath, watching the beads of perspiration forming along his brow, his heaving chest now glistening with moisture. Still, Jaime was unrelenting in his quest, picking up the pace, drawing him tighter, deeper into his mouth, his left hand tugging firmly on his balls as his right hand explored the damp surface of Tim's flat stomach and chest.

With a shout, Tim let go of the pent-up tension that had been welling within him for the past several months. He felt the rapturous release of his orgasm as he ejaculated into the warm, inviting shelter of Jaime's mouth.

After he came, Jaime continued to hold the spongy softness of his now-flaccid cock in his mouth, tasting the briny grit of him, like the finest sand of a beach or the most gentle of talcum powders. Jaime savored the taste before releasing the cock from the delectable prison of his mouth. Tim's penis lay like an inert, helpless bird between his muscular legs. Tim was looking down at Jaime tenderly.

"Thank you," he whispered almost inaudibly. Jaime rested his head on Tim's chest and listened to the steady beating of his heart, closing his eyes and relishing a closeness with Tim that he had never shared with another human being.

★ 18

Ruth placed the tabloid face up on her office desk. "I was afraid something like this was going to happen. If I've told you once, I've told you a thousand times to be ever watchful of the camera's lens. These pictures of you and your boy toy are pretty damning."

Tim picked up the tabloid and gave the front page a perfunctory glance before tossing it back on the desk. He had already seen the photographs of himself sharing a poolside clinch with Jaime on *Entertainment Tonight*.

"What do these pictures prove? They are pretty grainy and you can't even tell that it's me," he stated casually, displaying emotions that were on an even keel. Inside, however, he was furious that his privacy had been violated in such a public way.

"They don't have to prove anything, darling. In this town, you're presumed guilty, without the benefit of due process. You don't have to be convicted in a court of law for the damage to be done. The court of public opinion is far more influential. And this couldn't come at a worse time, what with the tabloids already in a tizzy over you breaking out of rehab. I'm too afraid to think about what the studio is going to say about this. I just hope that boy is a good enough lay to be worth the price you are going to pay."

Tim took extreme umbrage at Ruth's words. "Dammit, Ruth," he bellowed, raising his voice at her for the very first time. "Since when did you become such a judgmental ol' biddy?"

"I'll let that slip by, only because I know you've been under a great deal of pressure," she replied in a measured tone of voice. "You are in no position to get uppity with me, young man. I've watched you go from a naive greenhorn to one of the biggest stars in the world today. I've also watched you sabotage a wonderful relationship with David and potentially ruin your career and reputation. If I have to witness this train wreck you are causing, I'm damn sure not going to keep quiet about it," she told him.

Tim lowered his head and closed his eyes. "Ruth, I'm sorry. You are right, of course. You've been nothing but a friend to me over the years and I should be grateful to you for so many things. Please, accept my apology."

"Save your apologies, my dear. I'm an ornery old Jewish woman with leathery thick skin, so I can take whatever you want to throw at me." She laughed to lighten the mood, a deep, throaty laugh that conveyed all of her years of wisdom, as she had indeed seen it all in her lifetime. "David, on the other hand, is not as thick-skinned. I haven't heard from him today. I wonder if he's seen these yet?" she said, pointing to the tabloids.

"More than likely he has," Tim replied ruefully. "I have to meet with Dr. Janson at Milagros for another counseling session later this afternoon. I think I'll stop by and see David at his house before I go."

David answered the door wearing running shorts and an A-frame T-shirt, damp with the sweat from his daily jog along Malibu beach. He didn't appear too surprised to see Tim standing in his doorway.

"Hi," he said breezily, still out of breath from his jog. "I thought that I might hear from you today."

"May I come in?" Tim asked, relieved he hadn't slammed the door in his face.

"Sure, come on in."

As Tim walked into the house again, all of the happy memories the two had shared in the home came rushing back to him. He felt a lump forming in his throat but resisted it. "I thought that it was way past time for you and me to have a serious talk. David, we can't keep going on like this. I know that I am the one to blame for what happened, and I take full responsibility for my actions. I can't stand this tension between us anymore. Isn't there some way that we can resolve things?" he implored, searching his face for a sliver of sympathy.

"To be truthful with you, Tim, I've been a been a bit of a hypocrite. I don't have the right to stand in judgment of you when I'm not exactly a paragon of virtue. One thing I can say, though, is that I am a hell of a lot more discreet than you've been." An actual smile curled his lips, and Tim felt relief soar through his body.

"I take it you've seen the papers?"

David nodded. "Oh, yes, I have. I am curious as to where you met this guy. From the pictures, he looks to be quite young. Not normally your type, my dear."

"It's a long story, David. We don't have to get into all of the sordid details now. I have a counseling session with my doctor in a half hour. I just wanted to come by and seek your forgiveness. We've been through too much together to toss out our friendship. I want you in my life, David, always."

"You won't get rid of me that easily," David said, and they laughed and hugged each other like old friends.

"Where is he?" Raina demanded curtly as soon as Mariana had opened the front door.

"Good afternoon, Miss Hawthorne. If you are looking for Mr. Race, he is not here at the moment," Mariana replied, closing the door behind Raina.

"That figures. Is Jaime around?" she asked, removing her sunglasses and placing them in her Gucci leather handbag.

"I believe he is in the media room . . ." was all Mariana managed to say before Raina broke away, heading at a brisk pace in the direction of the media room.

She found Jaime playing a game of pinball, the machine clattering noisily, multicolored lights flashing. He was startled when Raina tapped him on his shoulder, and he spun around to face her.

"We need to talk."

Jaime inched his back closer to the pinball machine, looking like a timid gazelle trapped in a corner by a feral lioness moving in for the kill. "Hello, *Reina*." He pronounced her name as the Spanish word for *queen,* with the slightest trilling of the letter *r.* "Are you looking for Tim?"

"As a matter of fact, I was looking for Tim. Since he's not here, however, I think you and I should have a nice, private discussion." She reached into her handbag, pulled out several copies of the week's tabloids, and handed them to Jaime. "I thought perhaps these would be of interest to you."

He looked at the front cover of the tabloid in disbelief. "Who take these pictures?" His voice was a choked whisper.

"Some lucky photographer who just made a lot of money, I would imagine. But that's not important. I want to know what you intend to do about this."

Jaime looked back at her, not understanding. "What should I do?"

"Listen, Jaime. I realize that all of this must seem like a dream come true to you. What with living in a fabulous mansion and having Tim buy you beautiful, wonderful things, who wouldn't love it? What you don't see is that your relationship with Tim could prove to be very dangerous and destructive. Tim has so much more to lose here than you do. Do you understand what I am saying?"

Jaime nodded his head slowly. "Yes, I think I do," he said quietly.

"Good. I don't think it's a good idea for you to leave the house anytime soon. And definitely don't spend any time near the swimming pool. It would be best if you keep a very low profile, particularly over the next several weeks. By then, hopefully the press will have moved on to another target. In the meantime, just think about what I told you. I'm sure you are a nice person, Jaime. I know that you will do what is best for Tim, seeing how kind and generous he has been to you."

Raina turned to leave the room but stopped and looked back at Jaime. "As you know, Tim is an incredible man. Please don't do anything to destroy everything that he has worked so hard his whole life to achieve."

Jaime observed her as she left the room. He looked down at the tabloids that she had left behind and wondered how he had become a part of this strange, new world.

BOOK THREE:
THE DREAM FACTORY

September 2002, New York City

Anderson Garibaldi tipped the grateful taxicab driver twenty bucks. Why not? He was in a fantastic mood and the late-summer day was sunny and beautiful, a chamber of commerce spectacular.

He was scheduled to meet with his editor at the offices of Tribunal Publications in Dag Hammarskjold Plaza at one o'clock. That very morning, the prime minister of Canada had delivered a speech regarding the war on terrorism at the United Nations Building just across the street from his publisher's offices. Practically all of Midtown Manhattan had been caught in a nightmarish tangle of gridlock which, as luck would have it, cleared up just as he left his Greenwich Village loft near Washington Square less than twenty minutes before.

Anderson Garibaldi had made his name as the premier star biographer on the literary scene. Celebrities quaked in fear at the mere thought that Anderson would write a scathing tell-all revealing the most intimate secrets of their private lives. He had written blockbuster best-sellers about rock stars and royalty, actresses and serial killers, first ladies and business tycoons. It seemed that no one was safe from his poison yet golden pen.

Now, at the age of forty-one, his boyish good looks were still holding on with all of their might. He was short in physical stature but exuded an intimidating presence. As an openly gay man, he held a certain power that other gay men found attractive, and he used his fame and fortune to lure a neverending supply of beautiful, younger men into his lair.

He was quite excited about the proposal he had written for his upcoming biography. His last book, about a faded 1980s female pop star whose career in America had nosedived after she married an English director of misogynistic films, settled in Great Britain, and began bashing everything American, had been a disappointment in terms of sales. For his next book, he knew he would have to select a subject who would generate a great deal of interest—as well as sell a large quantity of books. The idea for the book came, innocuously enough, from a conversation he had in bed with his latest conquest.

Anderson had plotted and schemed for months to arrange a meeting with the hottest gay male porn star of the moment, a hunky slab of Grade A meat known only as Brutus. He had long been a fan of all-male, X-rated films, and he had met and seduced a number of the actors over the years. The relationships fizzled fairly quickly for the most part, as the actors usually burned out—from the sudden attention they received or from the rampant supply of drugs in the adult film industry—after a short while. The first time he saw Brutus, peering out at him seductively from a videocassette package and naked save for the bright orange hard hat he was holding over his privates, he knew he would one day have him in his bed.

Tall and tattooed, with cobalt blue eyes, bulging muscles, and blond hair, Brutus was an Adonis and had already developed an enormous following of adoring fans who thrilled at the sight of his ten-inch cock in action. On a trip to Los Angeles to meet with his West Coast agent, Anderson had called up Saulsalito Studios, the world's most prolific producer of gay adult films, and arranged a meeting with the brooding Brutus.

Brutus, né Bobby Taylor of Hot Springs, Arkansas, was all the things that Anderson appreciated in a lover: gorgeous, highly skilled with his cock, and not very bright. Anderson received more than enough intellectual stimulation from his work and people in the publishing industry; he had no use for it during his bedroom activities.

Anderson escorted Bobby, as he preferred to be called off camera, around town, paying for his meals in the nicest restaurants and showering him with expensive gifts. The sex was fabulous, as one might imagine, and Anderson did not mind the fact that Bobby's alter ego Brutus spent his days fucking other men; in actuality, that was part of the allure of sleeping with a porn star.

One evening, after having a few drinks at the celebrity-infested Sky Bar in the Mondrian Hotel on the Sunset Strip, they went back to Anderson's suite. After a rousing session of strenuous sex, they lay in bed, Anderson reading while Bobby channel surfed. The continuous clicking of the stations began to annoy him as he pored over material the PR director from the publishing house had sent by messenger to the hotel.

"Please, could you just stop on one channel and watch for a while?" he finally asked impatiently.

"Sorry. I didn't mean to disturb you," Bobby replied with the pout of a surly child.

The movie playing on the cable station he had at last selected was, fortuitously enough, *Death Never Waits*. After watching in silence for a few minutes, he suddenly turned to Anderson. "I slept with him, you know."

Anderson looked up from the paper he had been reading intently. "With whom?" he asked, suddenly very interested in what Bobby had to say.

"Tim Race, silly," he replied, a childlike grin on his face.

"You've slept with Tim Race?"

"Yeah. It was a couple of years ago, when I was working as a male escort. He paid me to come to his house and give him a massage. Of course, I gave him a massage and a whole lot more." He laughed lasciviously, the braying sound grating on Anderson's nerves.

"I can't believe that you actually slept with Tim Race. I mean, there have always been rumors that he was a member of the club, but . . ."

"Oh, he's a member of the club, all right. A card-carrying, full-fledged, and initiated member," Bobby said with a lewd wink.

"Please, continue. I want to hear everything and—for once—don't spare any of the details."

Bobby had told him of their exhausting sexual liaisons: what an attentive yet demanding lover Tim Race was and how much money he had paid him and what he paid him to do. Anderson was dubious about his story at first, but the more Bobby elaborated, the more convinced he became that he was telling the truth. And the story he was telling could potentially be worth millions of dollars to him.

Then, just last week, the tabloids had published the photographs of Tim sharing an embrace with a young, unidentified, Latino male companion. The timing had been impeccable. He had made certain to purchase as many of the tabloids as he could to bring with him to his meeting with his editor at Tribunal as interesting and entertaining visual aids.

He did not have to wait for his meeting with his editor; the secretary announced his arrival and was told to escort him immediately to the office.

"So, Anderson. How are things going with the new project?" Mitchell Kandinsky asked as soon as Anderson had taken a seat in his plush office with the sweeping views of the East River. Mitchell had been the editor in chief at Tribunal Publications for more than twenty-five years and was widely considered to be one of the most powerful and influential people in the publishing industry. He had been born into a wealthy and privileged New York family; his aunt was the incandescent actress Millie Obskaya, who had been one of the most famous stars of the silent-movie era. As well as being the editor at Tribunal, he had authored many best-selling potboilers under a nom de plume about Hollywood and moviemaking, a subject that enthralled him to this day. His most famous novel, *The Golden Silence,* was a roman à clef loosely based on the life of his indefatigable Aunt Millie and her rise to stardom during the Roaring Twenties, and included mentions of her rumored trysts with Valentino and Douglas Fairbanks.

"Things are going great, Mitchell. I suppose you've heard the latest gossip about Tim Race in the tabloids?" He reached into his Louis Vuitton valise and pulled out a copy of *The National Enquirer.* Mitchell took the newspaper and placed his reading glasses low on his nose to examine the cover.

"Very interesting," Mitchell said, browsing through the tabloid until he arrived at the four-page spread on Tim Race and his storied Hollywood career. "You know, I believe there's a book in here. There might even be a runaway *New York Times* nonfiction best-seller." He looked up at Anderson contemplatively. "I don't imagine you know of anyone who would be interested in writing such a book?"

Anderson chuckled and stood up from the chair, extending his hand across the desk. "I think I might," he responded as Mitchell shook his hand.

"How does a nice seven-figure advance sound to you, Anderson?"

"I'm a reasonable man, and that sounds like a very reasonable figure," he replied, his mind instantly calculating the profit he could conceivably earn and how many young, pretty boys he could subsidize with his tidy new bankroll, for he had already grown weary of Brutus.

"Very good." Mitchell pushed a button on his intercom console. "Patricia, please bring in a bottle of chilled Cristal champagne from the liquor cabinet and two champagne flutes. Mr. Garibaldi and I would like to toast his forthcoming blockbuster."

★ 20

Tim filled the specimen cup with urine, practically to overflowing. He had been holding it in for the better part of the day, and he sighed in relief at finally being able to empty his bladder. This would be the final drug screening; his requisite thirty days at the Milagros Center were now up. Drs. Janson and Westhall were very pleased with the progress he had made during his outpatient counseling. Both were more than happy to sign an affidavit detailing his good behavior to reassure the studio that he could now return to work on the much-ballyhooed *A Mission from Hell*.

"I'll take that." Nurse Robertson took the cup from Tim's hand as he exited the bathroom. "You have been one of our best patients, Mr. Race. I feel confident that you are more than ready to graduate from here."

Tim smiled at her, a smile that reflected his joy at having successfully completed the program. He would be able to report to work within the next several days, which he was anxious to do. Not working had made him antsy and restless. Not that there weren't enough diversions to keep him occupied. Chief among them was Jaime, whose innocent charm had already worked its way into his affections. Tim had not told anyone, not even Raina, that he was falling in love with Jaime. The truth was, he was too embarrassed to tell any of his friends about his true feelings for Jaime, out of fear that they would judge or repudiate him.

The door to the clinic room opened. Dr. Westhall entered, wearing his usual benevolent smile and cheerful countenance. "How are things with you today, Tim? I'm sure you are quite excited about leaving us."

"It's been nice, Dr. Westhall, but I think it's time that I move on and, hopefully, I won't have to return."

"If it doesn't sound rude, I hope you won't have a reason to visit us again either."

"That's all I need from you, Mr. Race," Nurse Robertson interrupted, placing a label on the urine specimen. "After this is tested and we get the results back, you can go back to work."

"Thank God," Tim replied, raising his hands in prayer.

"I'm home," Tim shouted from the foyer. Walking into the living room, he saw Jaime sitting on the floor, reading a letter.

"It's from my mother," Jaime explained as he carefully handled the rose-scented stationery. "She's in Florida now, living with my brother Mario. The money that you sent allowed her to bring all of my brothers and sisters to live in America too. She says that she is very proud of me . . ." His voice trailed off into tears.

"I'm so happy, Jaime. You must be so relieved to have your family safe and together now." Tim's voice was soft and caring.

"It's the nicest thing anyone could do for me, ever," Jaime whispered over his tears. "You are the kindest person I have ever known in my life."

"I'm not so great. I'm just trying to make up for so many of the bad things I've done over the years."

Jaime stared up at him questioningly. "You are not a bad person, Tim. I know that deep inside, you have the heart of an angel. I can feel your goodness here," he said, placing his hand over his own heart.

"I wish that I could believe that. Sometimes I don't feel so good about myself."

Jaime placed the letter carefully on the floor and stood up. "Believe it," he stated firmly.

Tim pulled him into his arms and kissed him on the top of his head. "God, you are so good for my ego."

"I only wish your friends would understand. Raina still does not like me very much. I don't think Ruth likes me either. And your friend David hates me, I think."

"I've already told you not to worry about them. And none of them hates you, Jaime. They are all just overprotective of me and they need to learn how to butt out of my life. At any rate, I'm inviting all of them to the birthday party I'm throwing for you next week."

Jaime's faced glowed in childlike anticipation. "I'm really going to have a birthday party! With presents and cake and everything!" he shouted ecstatically.

"Now what birthday party would be complete without cake and presents?"

The joyous sound of Jaime's laughter filled Tim's ears. "I can't wait to see what my present will be. I know that it will be something wonderful."

Their revelry was interrupted by the ringing telephone. Tim was hesitant to answer it, but he knew that it might be someone from the studio calling him to report to the set.

"Tim, we have a problem," David said gravely as soon as Tim picked up the phone. "Stay there. I'll be at your house in five minutes."

"So, what sort of recourse do I have here?" Tim asked David, his voice filled with righteous indignation.

"We'll have your lawyers file suit against this man, for defamation of character or for libel. We can also sue the German rag that published this preposterous story." David sifted through the pages that had been hastily printed off the Internet, translated from the original German magazine article. The story was just now breaking across the World Wide Web and into the English-language papers.

"I swear to you, David, I have never met this Brutus character in my life. This whole story about the two of us having an affair is a complete and total fabrication. You do believe me, don't you?"

"Yes, Tim. I believe you," David reassured. "I will have a discussion with your lawyers tonight. Then we'll make some sort of public announcement, denouncing the story printed in *Achtung!* magazine. This is another case of bad timing, what with the photographs of you and Jaime printed in the papers last month." David glanced over at Jaime, who was sitting alone in the corner, staring down at the floor. "The brouhaha about that was just beginning to die down, and now this."

The doorbell rang, and Mariana answered the door. Mariana was about to announce Ruth's arrival when Ruth beat her to the punch.

"I'm afraid I have even more bad news," she said soberly. "It appears that Anderson Garibaldi is currently writing a biography about Tim. I don't have to tell you what type of a sleazy muckraker this Garibaldi fellow is, now do I? He makes his living writing dirty exposés based on half-truths and capitalizing on scandals and rumors. One of his books almost cost the president the White House."

David placed his hand over his mouth and tapped the end of his nose with his finger. "Hmm. This is an interesting turn of events. I don't think that the German magazine article with the porn star and the fact that Anderson Garibaldi is writing a biography about Tim is a coincidence. Something tells me Garibaldi is behind this media stunt to draw attention to his book. This Brutus doesn't sound like he has the kind of brains to conjure up a story like this all on his own. The two must be in cahoots."

Tim raised his hands to his head and massaged his temples to calm the sudden, pounding headache he had developed. "I'm having a hard enough time keeping the truth about my life a secret. How in God's name can I fight the lies?"

"The truth, the lies, it's all the same thing in this town. Everything is just an illusion in the factory of dreams. It's the illusion you create for yourself that's the hardest to keep alive," David told Tim, a distant look in his eyes. Ruth nodded her head in agreement.

★ 21

The squawking sound of the alarm clock rocked Tim out of a deep, dreamless sleep. He had tossed and turned for most of the night before finally getting up and taking a handful of melatonin tablets, falling asleep at a little past three o'clock in the morning. The alarm had been set for seven o'clock, but Jaime had surreptitiously hit the snooze button three times so it was now almost seven-thirty.

"What time is it?" Tim asked, rubbing at his eyes.

"It's seven-thirty. I thought that you needed some extra sleep. You have been so tired lately," Jaime said, his hand caressing Tim's elbow that jutted out from beneath the quilted softness of the eiderdown duvet cover.

"Jaime, you knew that I had to be out of bed by seven. Now I'm going to be late for my first day back on the film set," he said testily, tossing the covers aside and jumping out of bed. He fished in the bureau for a fresh pair of underwear and grabbed a clean shirt from the walk-in closet.

"I am sorry. You have just been under so much . . . stress. I have been worried about you."

"And I appreciate that you care. It's just that it is very important that I show Mr. Whitmore and all the head honchos at the studio that I am dependable and back up to speed. They will all be watching me like hawks, seeing if I crack under the pressure."

"You will be fine. You are strong now. I see the difference in you," Jaime stated firmly. And it was true; he had noted a difference in the way Tim carried himself in the past several days since completing treatment at the rehabilitation clinic. He suspected that Tim was also happy that David was once again an important factor in his life.

"Let's just hope my strength holds me through the day," Tim said, picking up the script the studio had sent to the house, completely revised from the original script and with the addition of a new character to be played by Frederick van Nostrand. Only a few of the scenes already in the can were salvageable; most of the movie would have to be reshot at great expense to the studio, which was already grousing about Tim and Frederick's substantial paychecks.

"You'll be okay," Jaime said soothingly, brushing tiny particles of lint from Tim's shirt. "I will be thinking about you today." He bent his face upward to kiss Tim. "I love you."

The sudden admission startled Tim, who could not conceal the look of surprise on his face. He was certainly aware of an extreme fondness on Jaime's part toward him, and he had felt the stirrings of love inside as well. He had, however, decided not to move too quickly, not wanting to jeopardize their burgeoning relationship. He found the prospect of being in a new, loving relationship daunting, particularly after spending eleven years in a relationship with David.

At a loss for words, Tim simply smiled at Jaime and tousled his hair. "I had better get to the studio," he finally said. "I will call you this afternoon to let you know how things are going. Try not to get yourself into too much trouble today."

"I'll try not to," Jaime said, shaking his head and watching as Tim dashed out of the room and down the stairs. By now, he was accustomed to Tim taking flight whenever the topic of conversation turned to love or matters of the heart.

"Welcome back, Mr. Race. We haven't seen you around here in a while." The guard at the studio waved Tim through as the metal security gate rattled open, allowing Tim to guide the Mercedes onto the studio backlot.

It feels great to be back, Tim thought, feeling exhilaration mixed with apprehension at reporting to work again. He always felt happiest when he was working; work kept him focused and didn't allow his mind to wander. While working, he wouldn't have the time to worry about all of the rumors swirling around him or about the multi-million-dollar libel lawsuit being filed by his lawyers against Brutus, aka Bobby Taylor. One of the lawyers he had on retainer had advised him against filing the suit, saying that it would only bring more negative publicity. Another lawyer had said that he had no choice but to take the case to court, or other celebrities would be at risk of similar attacks. The truth was, Tim disliked dealing with anything litigious and tried to avoid a courtroom scenario whenever possible, which was difficult to do in a lawsuit-happy town like LA. He had an irrational fear of being on the stand with vicious lawyers interrogating him and prying into his closely guarded private life. On the witness stand, you were under oath and obligated to speak the truth. His publicist had released a statement vehemently denying the claims made by the disreputable Brutus and expressing, in no uncertain terms, that a lawsuit was imminent. The lawyers would also be seeking an injunction against Anderson Garibaldi and his upcoming book, although such measures were usually unsuccessful in blocking a book's publication. For the most part, the publicity only ensured the book would hit the best-seller lists. *Blasted First Amendment,* Tim thought angrily.

When Tim reported for duty at Studio A7, studio head Mr. Whitmore greeted him, surrounded by his posse of lawyers, accountants, and publicists.

"Good to see you again, Tim. I just wanted to let you know how pleased we all are that you have successfully completed treatment and that you reported for work on time, more or less," Mr. Whitmore said, looking at his watch. "Frederick van Nostrand is already here. He's in his trailer, going over the new script."

"Great," Tim responded, injecting a heavy dose of cheer into his voice and forcing himself to smile broadly. "I'm looking forward to working with Frederick."

"About all of this talk in the tabloids, Tim. I heard from a reliable source that you plan on filing a libel suit against this adult film star character. Are you sure that's the wisest choice?" Mr. Whitmore queried.

Tim felt himself shrinking before the omnipotent Mr. Whitmore. "My lawyers have been advising me, sir. I'm afraid I don't have any other recourse except to file suit. I simply cannot allow someone to go around spreading lies in the media about me, especially lies of this nature."

"I suppose you are right," Mr. Whitmore said heavily. "The damn lawyers must have their dirty fingers in every goddamn pie," he added, tossing a disdainful look over his shoulder. "But this business doesn't look very wholesome, you understand. We have a certain image we like to project around here. Anyway, just wanted to pop in and let you know how much we appreciate you around here, Tim. I'm very proud of you, son. Keep up the good work," he said encouragingly before walking off, his taciturn entourage trailing behind.

"So tell me. How are things going on the set of *A Mission from Hell?*" Raina asked, taking a bite of the organically grown celery she had brought with her, sealed in a baggie. The Nikki Haskell StarCaps diet was out and as she was on a new Hollywood fad diet that was all the rage. At least the emaciated, drug-addled waif look was out of vogue. She had called to arrange a lunchtime meeting at the studio commissary to get the latest scoop from Tim.

"Just swell. Mr. Whitmore made sure to be here bright and early to call me on the carpet about the lawsuit business. And Frederick van Nostrand's ego is about twice the size of the planet Jupiter. It's a wonder he doesn't have his own gravitational pull," Tim stated peevishly. "Things seem to be going from bad to worse in my life."

"I'm sorry, sweetheart. I had hoped our midday rendezvous would cheer you up."

"Just being with you always cheers me up. What's going on with you?"

Raina took a swig of her bottled water. "Well, I lost the part I was up for in that new comedy to Cameron Diaz. She seems to be getting all the good comedic roles these days. However, I was just sent a script for a movie about the life of Doris Day that I would kill to do. Cameron will probably land that one, too."

"You would be perfect as Doris Day," Tim enthused. "What are the chances that they would cast me as Rock Hudson?"

"That would certainly raise some eyebrows around here, now wouldn't it?" She laughed raucously. "We would make such an adorable couple. Speaking of couples," she segued, "where do things stand between you and David?"

"Being a bit obvious, aren't we?"

Raina feigned a look of innocence. "Obvious? You know perfectly well that I am a master of subtlety. I was just wondering if the two of you had progressed with the rekindling of your . . . *friendship*." She avoided Tim's gaze as she arranged the celery sticks on her plate in the shape of a square.

Tim looked at her knowingly. "We are again on speaking terms, if that's what you are asking. He's been my Rock of Gibraltar through this quagmire of bad press. And he's been supportive, more or less, of my relationship with Jaime. Wish I could say the same about some of my other friends, who shall remain nameless."

"I'll have you know that I have been nothing if not the supportive and devoted friend, so this guilt trip won't work on me. I'm sure Jaime must be a wonderful human being, although I fail to see how the two of you can form any sort of lasting relationship. But you know you always have my unconditional love and acceptance."

"Uh-huh," Tim said skeptically. "Friends forever. As such, you are cordially invited to attend Jaime's nineteenth birthday party, which I will be hosting next week at my house. Regrets only, please."

"So the boy is of the legal age of consent after all!" Raina exclaimed. "That is good news. What kind of present should I bring? Does he need a new high chair?"

Tim chuckled mockingly, enjoying the witty exchange of *Will & Grace*-like repartee that was the hallmark of their friendship. "You are just too funny! How Cameron Diaz is getting all the great comedy roles is beyond me."

Raina pulled a face. "Seriously. What should I bring for him?"

"I think a peace offering would be the best present he could receive from you."

"Didn't you know? I'm also a master at détente." She smiled at him blithely. "I wouldn't miss Jaime's little birthday soiree for anything in the world. Expect me there with bells on."

★ 22

The thirty-six-foot, fully equipped Airstream trailer parked on the studio back lot was visibly shaking, and Los Angeles was not experiencing an earthquake. The wardrobe assistant, standing some eight feet away from the rocking trailer, tried to act as if she didn't notice. She searched frenetically through the rack of clothes to pick out the outfit that had been marked with black felt swatches by the continuity department for Frederick van Nostrand to wear in the upcoming scene. Upon finding the proper combination of clothing, she took off and discreetly headed back toward the studio.

Inside the air-conditioned coolness of the luxury trailer, Tim was bent over a panting Frederick van Nostrand, who was kneeling on all fours on the Naugahyde love seat.

"Fuck me harder," he ordered sternly in his thick Dutch accent, his eyes tightly clenched and his face contorted into an unrecognizable scowl.

Tim pumped steadily into Frederick, who was thrusting his buttocks hard against him, causing the flesh on his ass to move in rippling waves away from the epicenter of impact. Tim had long been aware of the rumors about van Nostrand's alleged bisexuality, but such rumors circulated about *everyone* in show business. There had been gossip about him after his breakup with wife number four, an opportunistic former Miss America who had apparently told anyone who would listen that Frederick forced her into bisexual three-ways with his best friend, a ne'er-do-well, Eurotrash playboy. There was also talk of wild, Caligula-style orgies featuring copious amounts of drugs and some of the biggest names in Hollywood. He was often seen around town, carousing with his coterie of young, handsome male friends in his classic white Bentley. Once, he had been caught holding hands with one of his male companions outside of a club in West Hollywood. When confronted with the photographic evidence, he explained that it was simply a matter of cultural differences; heterosexual male friends often held hands and touched each other intimately while in public throughout Europe and it was completely acceptable behavior.

Even though he knew of the gossip regarding Frederick, Tim was nevertheless shocked when he had invited him back to his trailer, under the guise of doing a line reading for the next scene. Immediately after Tim entered his trailer, Frederick had pulled down his pants to expose his massive erection. Tim had not needed a formal invitation.

Frederick roared loudly as he reached orgasm. Tim continued to pump solidly until he pulled his cock out, ripping the condom off and tossing it aside. He masturbated himself to orgasm, shooting a thick stream of semen onto Frederick's buttocks and his sweat-covered back.

Tim tossed a clean linen towel to Frederick, who wiped away all evidence of their assignation. "Thank you," he said laconically. "Now, if you don't mind, I need to prepare myself for the next scene."

"You have messages here from Katie Couric, Barbara Walters, and Diane Sawyer. They are all desperately trying to land an interview with you regarding the lawsuit." Ruth handed Tim a stack of yellow Post-Its with messages written in bright red ink.

"Yeah, right. Like I want to talk about my private life with any of these broads," Tim said, tossing the messages into Ruth's metal wastebasket.

"These broads, as you so eloquently referred to them, have a powerful hold over public opinion. A twenty-million-dollar lawsuit tends to grab people's attention. An interview with any one of them could set things straight, once and for all."

"*Straight?* That's a curious choice of words."

"Oh, you know what I mean," Ruth said. "It might help your case if you appear on *Today* or *Good Morning America*. Moviegoers in Peoria watch those shows, you are aware."

"God, must I still pander to the fickle bigots that live in Peoria?"

"If you value your career, yes."

Tim knew that Ruth would eventually get her way; she always did. "Very well. Make the arrangements."

"I'd be happy to," she replied victoriously. "So, will it be Katie, Diane, or Barbara? Do you have a preference?"

"Surprise me."

"Don't I always, my dear?"

Later that afternoon, Tim called the house to make sure the preparations for Jaime's birthday party were going smoothly. David had enlisted the help of a reluctant Emilia to help Mariana with the cooking and cleaning. Emilia had become even more irascible over the years, if that was possible, and she still adored David but wasn't very fond of Tim.

Jaime had been so excited when he had said good-bye that morning. Tim had shrouded Jaime's birthday gift in a veil of secrecy. He had gone to a car lot the previous day to pick out the perfect car for Jaime, who needed his own set of wheels to tool around Los Angeles. Tim realized that Jaime was probably becoming bored, sitting around the house all day and waiting for him to return home from a long day on the set. When he saw the bright red Volkswagen Beetle, he knew that it was the ideal car for Jaime. He paid cash for it and was having it delivered that night, just in time for Jaime's birthday party. Of course, Jaime didn't have his license, at least not a legal one, but certainly there were ways around that minor detail.

Tim returned home to find Mariana still busy in the kitchen and a sullen Emilia dusting the gold-plated Oscar statuette and Golden Globe trophy showcased on the enormous fireplace mantel in the living room. A HAPPY BIRTHDAY, JAIME banner was draped across the keyhole-shaped doorway to the room. Tim had arranged for Jorge, the elderly gardener who came in three times a week to care for the estate grounds, to take Jaime with him on a shopping expedition for garden supplies in order to get him out of the house to prepare for the party. Mariana had baked a full-sheet chocolate birthday cake with butter cream frosting and nineteen ivory-colored candles. She had once worked for a bakery in her native country and was quite skillful at cake design. Mariana had recreated the Mexican flag on the face of the cake, complete with the red, white, and green panels and a fairly accurate rendering of the eagle devouring a serpent, a reference to Jaime's Aztec heritage. The Mexican motif continued outside by the pool, where the cake and refreshments were to be served. A giant piñata in the form of Quetzalcoatl, the mythical winged serpent of Aztec legend, was suspended from the portico entryway to the pool, brimming with delicious Mexican sweets.

Tim went upstairs to take a shower and to change his clothes. While he was in the shower, the images of his sizzling encounter with Frederick van Nostrand earlier that day filled his thoughts. He turned up the cold-water knob of the shower and allowed the icy bursts of water to purify his mind, body, and soul.

Raina was outside by the pool when he had finished with his shower and changed into fresh clothes. He was now wearing a pair of khaki trousers, a Panama hat, and a pair of leather Topsiders without socks.

"My, don't you look casual," Raina commented as he approached. She was wearing a knee-length, black knit Donna Karan skirt paired with a white silk blouse, unbuttoned just far enough to reveal her enviable cleavage and the tiny Maori symbol tattooed above her right breast, an homage to her New Zealand ancestry. Before leaving her house, she had slathered her pale, almost translucent skin in Clarins Sun Care Cream SPF 35 from head to toe. Botox injections notwithstanding, she had no intentions of becoming a leather-faced sun worshiper, à la Brigitte Bardot.

"I'm glad that you could make it. I trust you brought Jaime a present?"

She produced a small box from her handbag, swathed in an iridescent Mylar wrap and festooned with swirls of red ribbon. "You see, I can be a good and reliable party guest when I want to be. And where is your gift, pray tell?"

"It hasn't arrived yet. I was wondering if you had heard from David today?"

"No. Was I supposed to?"

"No. I was just curious, that's all."

"What have you been up to?" she asked slyly. "Have you been a bad boy?"

Tim rolled his eyes and scoffed. "I'm sure I don't know what you are talking about," he said casually, dipping a tortilla chip into a bowl of hot salsa and stuffing it into his mouth.

"Don't give me that, Tim Race. I can always tell when you have a guilty conscious about something or *someone*. Now, spill it. You know I'll weasel it out of you eventually."

Tim crunched loudly on the tortilla chip and chewed thoroughly before responding. "I swear, I can never keep any secrets from you. It's as if you can read my innermost thoughts."

"Spill it," Raina goaded. "Confession is always so good for the soul."

"I had sex with Frederick van Nostrand today," he blurted out quickly.

Raina gasped. "Oh, my Lord! Tim, you are such a little slut."

"Give me a break. He came on to me. Was I supposed to spurn Frederick van Nostrand's advances? He probably would have kicked my ass if I had."

"Jeez. Am I the only person in this town who isn't gay or doesn't swing both ways? Well, tell me. Was it any good?"

"Sure. It was fantastic. I mean, how could it not have been fantastic?"

"Touché. Does this mean you two are an item now and you will be giving Jaime the old heave-ho?"

Tim chortled at the thought. "Hardly. His ex-wife is still milking him for every penny he's worth in court. Look, I don't know why I had sex with Frederick. It was one of those one-shot deals. Or maybe it will just last until the end of filming. Who knows? Let's just keep this between the two of us, shall we?"

"Have I ever broken a confidence with you?" Raina asked, pretending to be offended.

"What are the two of you chattering about so conspiratorially?" David asked, approaching the two, a beautifully wrapped gift package in hand.

"Oh, Tim was just giving me the lowdown on Frederick van Nostrand, that's all," Raina said, giving Tim a wink.

"Really?" David replied, intrigued. "What's going on with Freddy?"

"The same old thing, I would imagine. Looks like he's set to lose his shirt to that scheming tramp of an ex-wife of his. She's really taking him to the cleaners," Tim covered. Raina secretly made an "a-okay" sign with her hand.

"You think he would have learned by now after being married so many times. He's a hardheaded European dolt, I would presume." David commented. "I hope I made it in time for the party?"

"You certainly did. Jaime's not back yet, but he should be here at any moment. Is Ruth able to make it?" Tim inquired.

"She said that she would. I hope you've taken precautions today. Are you sure there are no sneaky photographers snapping pictures of us at this very moment?"

"They haven't been bothering me too much lately. That strung-out rock star who beat up on his girlfriend last week has taken the attention away from me, at least for the moment."

"How fortunate for you," Raina chimed in. "David, do sit down and join us, please. You're straining my neck having to look up at you."

"Anything to make you more comfortable, Raina," David said snidely, taking a seat opposite Tim. "What did you get the birthday boy?"

"I guess I can go ahead and tell you guys," Tim said. "I bought him a new car, one of those adorable Volkswagens that look like tiny wind-up toys."

"How extravagant," was Raina's reply. "Does the boy even have a license?"

"Must you pooh-pooh everything? Jaime needs a car, so I got him one. I will kindly thank you to keep any disparaging remarks to yourself." He turned to David. "I suppose you are going to get on my case too?"

"I wasn't going to say a word," David responded. "It's your life; he's your boyfriend. You can do as you please."

"Hello, everyone," Ruth shouted as she approached the three. "There are two nice gentlemen out front that would like to deliver a new car to this address. You wouldn't know anything about that, would you, Tim?"

"Ruth, glad you could make it." Tim stood up to give her a kiss on the cheek. "Please, have a seat while I settle things with the car dealership." He strode away quickly, leaving the three to sit in an uncomfortable silence.

"God, what are we doing here?" Raina finally said, breaking the quiet. "This is all so ridiculous. Tim is off on another tangent with this *child* while we are all sitting around, doing nothing."

"What would you suggest we do?" David asked.

"I don't know. What I do know is this *relationship* with Jaime, if that's what you want to call it, is going to cause Tim nothing but heartache if it continues."

Ruth spoke up. "Listen, I care about Tim as much as you two, but we don't have a right to interfere with his personal life. We may have our own opinions, but we should just keep them to ourselves. I, for one, believe the relationship with Jaime will come to a natural end once Tim comes to his senses and gains some perspective about his life and the path he's taking. We should just stand back and let Tim learn from experience," she advised.

"And what happens if he doesn't learn, Ruth? What happens if we stand by and do nothing and he ends up ruining all the things he has worked so hard to achieve?" Raina demanded. "What then?"

"Then we'll be around to pick up the pieces, like the caring, loving friends we are," David replied.

When Jaime returned with Jorge, he burst into tears at the beautiful party decorations and the scrumptious cake Mariana had baked especially for him. He tore into the presents David, Ruth, and Raina had bought for him with the frantic anticipation of a young boy on Christmas morning. Raina's porcelain figure of the Temple of the Sun in Tenochtitlan, Mexico, which she had purchased from a flea market in a dangerous section of East LA, was of particular value to Jaime, who viewed the gift as a sign of her acceptance of him in Tim's life.

It was Tim's gift, however, that brought Jaime the most joy. When Tim handed him the keys and showed him the Volkswagen Beetle, wrapped in a massive white bow, he could not believe his eyes.

"You do know how to drive, I hope?" Tim asked, sliding into the passenger seat of the manufacturer-fresh automobile.

"Yes. Not very good, but I can drive," Jaime assured him.

"Hope you have more than liability insurance, Tim," Raina said.

"So, you do like your gift?" Tim asked.

"It's the most wonderful thing anyone has ever bought for me," Jaime replied, leaning in to give Tim a kiss as David, Raina, and Ruth looked on in stony silence.

December 2002

Upon completion of filming *A Mission from Hell,* the cast and crew gathered for a postproduction/pre-Christmas bash, hosted by Mr. Whitmore's lovely blonde trophy wife, Sabrina. Tim, for one, was ecstatic that filming was finally completed and that everything had gone off without a hitch. Mr. Whitmore congratulated Tim on a job well done, and he felt confident that the movie would rake in more than $200 million at the box office. It was a feat that all of his movies had accomplished, with the exception of the esoteric drama *Weak Are the Kind,* which earned only $150 million globally, a somewhat minor disappointment.

Frederick van Nostrand attended the wrap party with his latest girlfriend, a cute, young assistant script supervisor from the film, who boasted in a haughty manner that she would be accompanying Frederick on his trip to Tokyo to film a credit card commercial for Japanese television. Most Hollywood stars would never deign to do an advertisement for American television, but were only too eager to accept the scads of yen Japanese companies tossed their way to hock their wares. Tim shook Frederick's hand cordially before he left. The two had met clandestinely several more times during the course of filming—usually in his or Frederick's trailer—for quick, hot sex and nothing more. Frederick wished him the best of luck before ducking out of the party early, his young girlfriend in tow.

At the party's close, Tim felt the usual anticlimactic emotions associated with the end of another project. He had made sure to give his all to his performance in the film, knowing that his credibility with the studio was contingent on the film's success. On the home front, things had progressed smoothly in his relationship with Jaime, and his friends were gradually coming around in their acceptance of him. The truth of the matter was he felt strong and good about himself whenever he was around Jaime. He was great for his ego, and it had been a long time since he had felt so at peace with himself.

Jaime had made an effort to achieve his own self-reliance since Tim had purchased the car for him. He had insisted Tim give him driving lessons, mostly in the driveway to the house, but they had ventured out onto the streets of Bel Air on more than one occasion. Once, Jaime had accidentally knocked over a collection of garbage containers at the end of the neighbor's drive, and the two had laughed hysterically as Jaime sped away from the scene of the crime. He was only slightly concerned about his illegal immigrant status; he always felt safe when he was in Tim's company. He knew that Tim would never allow anything bad to happen to him.

In the weeks before Christmas, a flurry of activity took place at Tim's house. A magnificent, twenty-foot Norwegian pine was shipped in from upstate New York and placed in Tim's den. Mariana helped Jaime and Tim decorate the tree. Strategically placed mistletoe had Tim and Jaime stopping to kiss every few minutes, to the delight of a giggling Mariana. A plethora of presents were quickly placed beneath the tree, and Jaime examined each one that bore his name carefully, trying to guess its contents.

It would be a different Christmas than those Tim had experienced over the past few years. David had already made plans to visit his parents at their Nob Hill estate in San Francisco over the holidays, while Raina was set to jet off to Auckland to spend Christmas with her family.

Ruth did not disappoint, however, continuing her annual ritual of spending the final night of Hanukkah with Tim, where they somberly lit the menorah together. Jaime was deeply inquisitive about the Jewish celebration, and Ruth educated him with an abundance of information on her religion. Tim's eyes twinkled as he watched one of his oldest, dearest friends explain with reverence the symbolism of the menorah to an eager-to-learn Jaime over cups of nonalcoholic, calorie-laden egg nog, which Jaime gulped down by the gallon.

On Christmas Day, Jaime was delighted to receive a telephone call from his mother in Florida. They chatted away for hours, catching up on all the things that had happened since the last time they spoke. All of his brothers and sisters were acclimating to their new lives in America, and Lorena had found a good-paying job at a pleasant, well-run factory that did not exploit immigrant labor. They said their goodbyes with Jaime's promise to visit her in Florida soon. It made Tim feel proud that he had been able to help Jaime's family in such a way. Although he donated large sums of money to charity each year, he often felt as if he wasn't doing his share to help the less fortunate people in the world.

After opening all of the gifts, they sat beneath the sparkling Christmas tree, admiring the beautiful decorations and enjoying the peace and quiet of their time together.

"Are you happy, Jaime?" Tim suddenly asked.

Jaime craned his head around to look up at him. "Yes, Tim. I am very, very happy."

"That makes me happy," he said, planting a soft kiss on the top of Jaime's head.

"Happy New Year, my love!" Raina shouted over the telephone.

"Thank you. But it isn't New Year here yet," Tim said.

"Well, it is already New Year's Eve here in New Zealand. You are aware of time zones, are you not?"

"I think I've heard of them before," he said. "I'm sure you must have had a fabulous Christmas Down Under with all of your clan."

"Indeed. As you know, this is a working holiday for me. Most of my latest film is being shot on the South Island, which is truly awe-inspiring. I think the main reason I signed on to do this movie was for the free trip to Kiwi country."

"You sound in good spirits. It's been a while since I've heard that effervescent inflection in your voice."

"What can I say but absence makes the heart grow fonder. I'm missing you again. How did you and Jaime spend your Christmas?" Raina asked, her voice free of the usual edge it held when she spoke of Jaime.

"Just a quiet celebration, here at the house," he answered. "Actually, it was one of the nicest Christmases I've had in recent memory."

"That's great to hear. I was a little concerned, what with both David and I abandoning you over the holidays. From the sound of things, you no longer need either one of us in your life."

"Don't be ridiculous, Raina. I don't even want to think about not having you or David in my life. Now, when are you getting your arse back to LA?"

Raina laughed breezily. "In a few week's time. Think you can make it that much longer without me?"

"I'll try and survive, as hard as it might be."

"Do you have any plans for New Year's Eve?"

"Not really. I think I'll spend a quiet evening here at the house with Jaime."

"Sounds like an outrageously good time," she replied drolly. "Try not to party too hard."

"Life isn't all about parties and having a good time, you know. There are moments in one's life where you search for something more meaningful," Tim said.

"I know what you mean." Raina suddenly found herself fighting back tears, an emotion she had not anticipated, and she forced a note of joyousness in her voice. "I have to go, my love. It's a brand new year and I have about fifty resolutions to start breaking. Happy New Year!"

"Happy New Year to you as well. I love you very much."

"Ditto. Ciao."

"Ciao, friend," Tim said softly.

Just before midnight on New Year's Eve, Tim and Jaime stepped out onto the balcony from his bedroom to enjoy the coolness of the evening. The neighborhood was quiet, but the sounds of celebration could be heard from across the distance. Tim had brought with him a bottle of champagne and two chilled flutes, the frostiness of the glasses turning the tips of his fingers numb.

"I would like to propose a toast," Tim said, popping the champagne cork, which ricocheted off the wall and landed on the table before them. Streams of white foam sprang forth from the bottle before Tim was able to fill the flutes up with the bubbling liquid. "To life, love, and the pursuit of happiness. Happy New Year, Jaime."

Jaime raised his glass to clink it gently against Tim's. *"Salud,"* he said, the traditional toast meaning good health.

Tim echoed Jaime's toast before lifting the glass to his mouth and drinking down the champagne in one quick gulp. "Ahh," he sighed. "Go ahead. Drink your champagne."

Jaime hesitantly put the glass up to his mouth. He took a tiny sip. Tim encouraged him to drink it all down. Jaime tilted his head back and wolfed the champagne, shaking his head upon finishing because he was not accustomed to the taste.

Tim laughed heartily. "That was great. Now, we must continue with the tradition of tossing our glasses and breaking them," he said. He then lifted the flute up high above his head before tossing it to the floor. It crashed against the Spanish tiles and shattered into thousands of microscopic shards of glass, which scattered across the balcony. Tim laughed again. "Now it's your turn. Go ahead, throw your glass."

Jaime grinned broadly as he eyed the glass in his hand. He tossed the flute high into the air, watching it do graceful somersaults before landing on the floor and smashing noisily. The sound of the breaking glass echoed across the yard and against the rooftops of the neighboring houses.

Tim clapped his hands. "That's the spirit. Life is about doing the unexpected, taking a risk and going against the grain. These are the things that make life worth living." He was staring at Jaime seriously. "Being with you the past several months has made my life worth living again."

Jaime was momentarily caught off guard. He felt tears forming in his eyes but fought to quell them. "You know that I love you, Tim. I would do anything to make you happy."

"You do make me happy, Jaime. I didn't know that I would find this sort of happiness with someone again. I wanted to tell you . . ." he paused to take a breath. "I wanted to tell you that I love you, too."

Trembling, Jaime pressed his hands to Tim's face, caressing the expanse of his high cheekbones and tracing the outline of his lips. Tim brought his fingers into his mouth and kissed the palms of his hands. Their lips joined together, finally and passionately, just as the grandfather clock in Tim's room struck midnight. Their kiss was full of promise, a hopeful harbinger of the year to come.

★24

"I can't believe you don't want to attend the Oscars this year," Raina exclaimed. "Who the hell am I supposed to take then?"

"I don't know. There really is no point in me attending this year. It's not like I received a nomination and am obligated to go. Besides, I've had nothing but bad luck since winning last year," Tim said, not looking up from the *New York Times* crossword puzzle he had been working on studiously for over an hour.

"That's superstitious rubbish and you know it. If you don't go, I'm in a bind. All the other great catches are taken. Brad and Ben have their own respective Jennifers. Harrison has Calista, not that I'm looking for a daddy figure. Reese has that yummy piece of eye candy Ryan Phillippe, the lucky girl. Jude has Sadie; Duchovny has Téa. Tom has Penélope and Antonio has the overpossessive Melanie. I wonder who Heath Ledger is dating now? Is he still with Naomi? You know how I am about studly Australian men."

"Trust me, I haven't forgotten. Especially after the way you threw yourself at a brooding Russell Crowe during the Golden Globes last year."

Raina elected to ignore his comment. "I've arrived at the conclusion that being with you has put a definite crimp in my sex life. I might as well become a celibate nun—I'm not getting any nookie. And you refuse to give it up. It's like I'm persona non grata with the opposite sex these days. Thank God for my vibrator. I bought it at the Pleasure Chest and it has variable speeds and these wicked attachments and I give it a real workout, believe me." Raina made an exaggerated buzzing noise.

"I believe you, so please, spare me the details," Tim begged.

"Matt Damon!" she shouted, clapping her hands. "Do you know how to get in contact with Matt?"

"Try Ben's house," he teased.

Raina sighed her disappointment. "You are absolutely no help whatsoever, you know. To think of all the things I have done for you over the past decade. You should be ashamed of yourself for not caring about me or my happiness."

"All right, all right! I acquiesce. You will just badger me relentlessly until I agree to go with you to the Academy Awards. So save your breath: I'll go with you! Besides, with this lawsuit business still hanging in the air like some noxious cloud, I need to be seen out on the town with a lovely lady such as yourself."

"Yippee!" she squealed, jumping up and dancing around the room. "We'd better start making plans. How about we show up in matching Versace outfits, like Will Smith and Jada Pinkett Smith?"

"Don't you think that's a bit too," he searched for the proper word, " . . . *precious?*"

"Perhaps you're right. I should go. So many details to tend to, and of course I, being the female, must take care of practically everything."

"I know. That's why I chose you to be my best friend."

Tim found Jaime in the garden, helping Jorge plant a fresh batch of petunias. Jaime enjoyed working outside with Jorge because he reminded him so much of his father, whom he still missed terribly and thought of every day. Puttering about in the garden was relaxing for him and it gave him something to occupy his time.

"You look right at home working in the garden," Tim remarked to Jaime, who was on his knees digging into the dark, rich soil with a garden trowel.

"I like this. I used to help my mother and father plant the crops in Mexico. We never had to buy fruits and vegetables from the market. It makes me feel at home."

"You are obviously doing a great job. Isn't that right, Jorge?"

The elderly man smiled a toothless smile at Tim and laughed. He then continued on with his planting.

Jaime noticed that Tim had changed clothes. "Are you going out today?"

"I thought that I might. I've been sticking close to home for the past several weeks and I have a touch of cabin fever. You'll be okay here for the rest of the day, won't you?"

"Sure. I think Jorge wants me to help him trim the row of shrubs bordering the swimming pool. Have a nice time."

"Thanks. Take it easy and don't let Jorge work you too hard," Tim said as he walked away, whistling the opening melody to Michael Jackson's "Beat It."

Tim pulled up to the dark-haired youth on a side street between La Cienega Boulevard and La Brea, just south of the Santa Monica Freeway. He had observed him for more than a half hour, and in that time frame he had already serviced one middle-aged businessman wearing a suit and tie and driving an Audi. Tim was pretty sure the guy wasn't working for the vice squad.

"Hey there. Are you still on duty?" he asked the young man, who resembled a rougher-looking version of Sal Mineo in *Rebel Without a Cause,* only with a buzz cut and multiple gang tattoos.

"What's it to ya?" the youth asked.

"A couple hundred bucks," he replied matter-of-factly.

"You ain't no fuckin' cop, is you? 'Cause if you is, I might have to get ghetto-style on your ass." His speech was slurred, courtesy of a new tongue stud.

Tim pulled up his shades to rest on top of his head. "Do I look like a cop to you, boy?"

The young man whistled. "Fuck! You's that actor, Tim somebody or the other. You like that freaky queer stuff, does you?"

"Do you want to shoot the breeze or do you want to earn some money?"

"If you pays me enough to show some bling-bling around town, we can talk business. I likes to keep my hos in high style."

Tim noticed the teardrop tattoo just below his left eye. "What gang are you running with?"

"What do you know about gangs, Mr. Hollywood? You wouldn't know the difference between one of the Alley Boyz or a Big Top Loco, so what chu talkin' about, fool?"

"Fair enough. So, are you interested or not?"

The dark-haired youth lifted up his shirt to reveal his muscled, tattooed stomach. The word *playa* was etched in large, black lettering across the entire width of his abdomen. He also revealed the handle to his Beretta M9 semiautomatic pistol, peeking out from beneath his baggy Tommy Hilfiger boxer shorts.

"Let's get it on, faggot," the youth said. He reached down to open the door.

Instinct and common sense suddenly took hold of Tim, who quickly pushed the automatic locking mechanism to the doors and rolled up the window. Out of the corner of his eye, he saw an obsidian gleam as the man pulled out the gun and pointed it directly at him through the glass. Tim pressed hard against the accelerator and in an instant was roaring away from the curb. The sound of gunfire rang out, but Tim did not stop. He looked into the rearview mirror until he could no longer see the man with the gun. He didn't stop until he reached a red light several blocks away, where he pulled off the street and parked in front of a convenience store. Tim remained there until his hands had finally stopped shaking and his breath and heart rate had at last returned to normal.

★ 25

Jaime watched Tim intently as he shaved. He enjoyed watching him perform his daily ablutions, hypnotized by the sight of the cold steel of the razor gliding gently across the harsh stubble of his whiskers.

Tim caught Jaime staring in the bathroom mirror and turned to smile at him as he sat on the toilet seat. "I wish you could be with me tonight."

Jaime's expression turned downcast and he looked away. "I know that I can't be with you in front of the entire world. You are too ashamed of me."

"You know that isn't the reason why. I've explained all of this to you before. You understand the way it has to be."

"I know, I know. I'm sure Raina is quite happy about going with you to the Oscars tonight, isn't she?"

"I'm sure she is excited. We go together every year. It's sort of our annual tradition. She'd be heartbroken if I blew her off," Tim explained, dunking the razor in hot water.

"You will look very handsome. The two of you together will make a beautiful couple."

"Could you bring me my tuxedo, please?" Tim asked. Jaime entered the bedroom and brought back the Versace tuxedo, the cummerbund and tie matching the color of Raina's couture gown. She had finally selected a creamy yellow, off-the-shoulder dress designed by Gianfranco Ferré with matching jewelry provided by Harry Winston. Joan and Melissa Rivers had given her rave reviews on the red carpet for the past three years running, and she wanted to continue with her sartorial winning streak.

Jaime helped Tim into the tuxedo. He lovingly buttoned up the freshly starched shirt and assisted Tim with his twenty-four-karat gold cufflinks. Once he was in full regalia, Jaime looked at him admiringly.

"You will be the most beautiful-looking man there tonight," he predicted.

"I'm sure there will be plenty of others better-looking than me," Tim replied.

"Not to my eyes."

Tim stroked his face and brushed his bangs, which had grown shaggy once again, from his eyes. "Be a good boy tonight while I'm gone," he whispered softly in his ear.

"I promise. Now you promise me the same."

Tim smiled widely. "I solemnly do promise to be a good boy tonight," he said, lifting up his right hand and placing his left over his heart.

The scene at the shiny new Kodak theater was the familiar madhouse of Oscars past. Tim and Raina strutted their stuff before the multitude of cameras, broadcasting their images to more than a billion people around the globe. The pressure was off, for neither Tim nor Raina was up for an award, so they were free to enjoy the festive atmosphere. Superstars made their way along the red carpet, stopping intermittently to schmooze with fellow celebrities or members of the international press.

While the ceremony itself was the focus of most of the media attention, the postceremony bashes were truly the hottest tickets in town. Immediately after the last award had been handed out, Tim and Raina made a beeline to the exit. They had tickets to the most coveted invite in town: the *Vanity Fair* post-Oscar party held at Morton's restaurant on Melrose Avenue in West Hollywood. There were other parties in town, for sure: the Governor's Ball, catered by Wolfgang Puck, where actors and directors meshed with important politicos and Washington pundits; the rowdy Elton John AIDS Foundation party, where the flamboyant rock star delighted friends and followers alike with his antics and earned millions of dollars for charity. The *Vanity Fair* party, however, was still considered to be the ultimate in chic.

Tim and Raina split up upon arrival at party headquarters. Raina was off to huddle with the cast of *Sex and the City* while Tim was cornered by his old buddy Talbot Grayson, whom he had not seen in several years. Raina was snapped in a cozy position with Heath Ledger, sans his latest girlfriend, continuing her tradition of lusting after unavailable Australian men.

In the midst of all the craziness, Tim's cell phone rang. He reached in and grabbed it from his breast pocket, ducking away to a relatively quiet corner to answer. "Hello," he halfway shouted into the phone.

"Tim? Tim darling?" a familiar voice asked.

"Mama? Is that you?" Tim said in bewilderment.

"Yes, dear. It's your mother here. I know it's been a long time, but . . ." her distant voice broke off. "I called that nice David fellow that works for you and he gave me your cell phone number. I told him it was an emergency. Tim, you need to know that your father is real sick. I've wanted to call you before now, but he wouldn't let me, the pigheaded fool that he is. Oh, please forgive me, Lord. Son, your father is . . . dying. I think you should come home to Tenpole before he passes on."

Tim was dumbstruck. "Daddy's dying?"

"Yes, honey. I know that things ain't never been right between the two of you, but I don't think you want your father to pass on to another world without having the opportunity to say good-bye or maybe to make amends. I want you to know that your daddy is proud of you, even if he never told you. I found a scrapbook in his dresser drawer after he became ill, and it has nothing but magazine and newspaper clippings about you and your career out there in Hollywood. You should know that I am proud of you too, son."

"Do you think Daddy would really want me to come and see him?"

"He'd never admit it in a million years, but I know he would love to see you. You are his only son. Please, won't you come?" Deanna pleaded.

"I'll be there as quickly as I can."

★ 26

Carl James Gividend died on a peaceful Easter Sunday morning. Tim had caught the red-eye out to Dallas within hours after his mother's urgent telephone call. Carl was in the final stages of terminal colon cancer and had lapsed into a coma. Tim had stood by his hospital bed and held his father's hand. Carl opened his eyes for a brief moment and gently tugged on Tim's hand, as if in recognition, before closing his eyes again and drifting back into unconsciousness. He remained in a coma for almost four weeks. Tim had returned to Los Angeles, commuting back to Texas each Friday to be with his father. Jaime had wanted to go with him, to console him and offer him support, but that was out of the question, of course.

Deanna and Tim mutually decided that it would be best to turn off the life support, for Carl would not have wanted to live out the remainder of his life in such a state. Tim made sure that he was there when the doctors switched off the breathing apparatus. He watched stoically while the life drained from his father, who was virtually unrecognizable; he had dwindled down to less than one hundred pounds and the continuous morphine drip used to control the overwhelming pain had turned his skin a deathly shade of ash. No buzzers announced his father's death, no flashing lights or sirens or host of doctors and nurses swarming about. That existed only in the overwrought melodrama of television shows and movies. In the dismal solitude of the hospital room, his father's passing had a quiet dignity.

Deanna and Tim held Carl's hands as he drifted away from this world. The doctor nodded grimly and noted the time of death. The nurse and doctor left Tim and his mother to say their final good-byes before the body was wheeled away. Only then did Tim release his emotions. He cried, not so much tears of sadness at his father's death, but rather for all the time that had been wasted. He never knew his father, nor did his father ever know him. They had been virtual strangers in the world. Tim felt anger and frustration as well; anger that his relationship with his father had tainted all of his other relationships in life. Was he the way he was because of how his father had treated him? In the end, Tim realized he was culpable for his own actions. It was unfair to blame his father for how he had turned out in life. He was a grown man, after all, with freedom of choice. He had chosen of his own volition to live his life in a certain way, and if things had not always gone as planned, he could not place all of the blame on an itinerant and emotionally detached father.

His mother embraced him as they watched Carl being wheeled from the room. "I am sorry, son. I am sorry that you didn't have the opportunity to form a lasting, loving bond with your father. I only pray that your father is at peace with himself and that he is in the arms of Our Lord now."

"Mama, do you think Daddy ever loved me?" he asked tearfully, his voice breaking with emotion.

"In his own way, son. Yes, I believe he did. I believe he loved us both in the only way he knew how."

His mother's heartfelt words offered him the tiniest morsel of solace.

Raina arrived in Tenpole early on Monday morning. She rented a Toyota Corolla at the airport in Dallas and made the two-hour drive to Tenpole, deep in the armpit of nowhere, in an hour and fifteen minutes flat. She pulled up to the red-shuttered double-wide trailer just as Tim's mother's flapjacks were cooking on the griddle, the delicious scent wafting on the warm, spring breeze.

"What's that wonderful smell?" she asked, knocking on the screen door.

"Raina! You didn't have to come, you know!" Tim said, opening the door and pulling her into his arms. He had told her over the phone that he would be perfectly fine, but she could detect the tone of sadness in his voice and knew he wanted her with him, whether or not he told her in so many words.

"Where else would I be but here with you? Especially now. So how are you holding up?"

"Better, now that you are here."

Tim introduced Raina to his mother, who was delighted to see that her son had a female companion. She served them both heaping plates of pancakes, smothered in butter and homemade boysenberry syrup, along with scrambled eggs and country-cured ham. They greedily attacked the food, Raina, for once, not counting calories.

"She's in love with you, you know," Deanna told him once Raina had excused herself from the table to use the bathroom.

"Who, Raina? Oh, we're just two very dear old friends. We've been through so much together over the years."

"It's obvious, Tim. I can see the love in her eyes when she looks at you. You can't mistake the look of a woman in love. I thought that perhaps you would like to settle down one day soon with someone beautiful and charming like her. Wouldn't it be nice to have a wife and to start a family? You're at that age, my son. The folly of youth is behind you and it's time to start thinking about laying down some roots. I realize that Hollywood isn't exactly a place where family values and morals are revered or appreciated, but still. And I'm just dying to have some little grandchildren to love in the proper way. I might be able to make up for all of the mistakes I made with you."

He didn't know what to say. He had thought about this often over the years. The idea of having a family appealed to him, but it never seemed to be in the cards for someone in his position in life.

"Mrs. Gividend, those pancakes sure were delicious," Raina said after she had returned from the bathroom. "I can't remember the last time I enjoyed my breakfast so much."

"Thank you, my dear. And please, call me Deanna."

"How about if I just call you Mom?" Raina crinkled her nose sweetly at Tim.

"Raina, that has a mighty lovely sound to it," she replied, removing her apron and smiling affectionately at her son.

David called from Los Angeles that afternoon.

"Tim, I'm so sorry about your father. Is there anything I can do for you?" David asked.

"No, but thank you for caring. It's been a rough couple of days. Raina has been a godsend."

"That's one of her greatest gifts. She could always make you feel better by just being around you. The two of you share a rare, cosmic bond, kind of like you were separated at birth. Actually, I had another reason for calling you. I spoke with your lawyer a short while ago, and he says that the German conglomerate that owns *Achtung!* magazine is willing to make a settlement out of court in the libel suit."

"That is good news. Tell him to accept whatever they offer. Then take what's left after the lawyers deduct their share and make an anonymous contribution to both the Anti-Defamation League and the Elizabeth Glaser Pediatric AIDS Foundation. I want to drop the libel suit against Bobby Taylor. I think I've made my point. It's time to move on with my life. And if Anderson Garibaldi wants to expose all of my secrets—so be it."

"It sounds as if you are at a crossroads yet again. Anything I can help you sort out?" David offered.

"You've done more than enough for me, David. I wouldn't be who I am without your love and guidance."

"I'll always care about you. Nothing will ever change that, Tim."

"Can I ask you a favor, then?"

"Anything for you," David said.

"Can you check in on Jaime for me? I've been worried about him over the past few weeks. He's been rather withdrawn from me lately, especially since my father became ill. I don't think he was very happy that I wouldn't let him come to Texas with me. Do you mind popping in and seeing that he's doing okay?"

"You really do love him, don't you?"

"More than I could have ever realized," Tim said thoughtfully.

"I'll drive over to your house and see him this afternoon," David promised.

"Thank you, my dear and wonderful friend. I love you."

★ 27

Mariana did not recognize the man standing at the front door. Her eyes were wide with concern; this strange man had obviously circumvented the security system or he would not have been able to gain entry to the house. She inched her right hand closer to the panic button near the door that Tim had installed immediately after the September 11 attacks on the nation.

"Miss, I hope I didn't startle you," the man said. "Mr. Race is expecting me. I realize that he is in Texas due to the death of his father, but he was insistent that I come to the house today and take care of this business right away."

"Mr. Race did not inform me that there would be any visitors here today," Mariana replied suspiciously. "Mr. Race informs me of *everything* that goes on in his house."

"I do not doubt that for a second, Miss. I'm sure that Mr. Race just forgot to mention it, considering what he has been through over the past several days." The man lifted up his attaché case to prove that he had legitimate business at the house. "I could come back later, after you have spoken with Mr. Race. I just hope he isn't inconvenienced by this little situation."

Mariana thought about the displeasure Mr. Race would feel at being interrupted while he was mourning the death of his father, especially over something petty and trivial.

"You sure you are not one of those pesky reporters that have been sniffing around here?" she demanded.

"A reporter? Oh, good heavens, no. I am an assistant to his lawyer, Derek Jacoby. This is regarding the lawsuit with the German magazine. Mr. Race told me that there was some pertinent information regarding the case here at the house, and he asked me personally to come over and pick it up for him. He gave me the access codes to the gate, you see. I just need to go to the library and retrieve the information and take it back to Mr. Jacoby."

Mariana eased her hand away from the panic button. "I see. That would be fine, then. Please, come in. You do know where the library is, do you not?"

"If you would be so kind as to show me the way," he replied.

"Follow me, Mr. . . . what did you say your name was?"

"Mr. Standish. Barry Standish."

Mariana escorted him to the library. "This is Mr. Race's personal library. I will wait for you here while you find the documents that you are looking for."

"Of course," the man said understandingly. "It will take but a moment."

Mr. Standish went immediately to Tim's oak escritoire. He lifted up a manila envelope that was labeled "Barry Standish" in bright red lettering. "I believe this is what I came for," he said, walking toward Mariana and showing her the envelope bearing his name.

"Very well, sir. I'll show you out."

"Actually, Mr. Race asked me to do something else while I was here. He said that I needed to speak with a Jaime Adame. It is a matter of great confidentiality. Do you know where I might be able to find Mr. Adame?"

Mariana was surprised that this stranger knew of Jaime's presence in the house. "I saw Jaime earlier. He was working outside with Jorge the gardener, but I think he went up to his room to take a shower a little while ago. If you will follow me, I will show you to his bedroom."

Mariana rapped lightly on the bedroom door. "Jaime? Are you in there?"

Jaime opened the door with a broad smile on his face. He was shirtless and wearing the faded pair of blue jeans that he always wore when he worked in the garden. He registered a look of concern when he saw the man standing behind Mariana.

"Jaime, this is Mr. Standish. He works for Mr. Race's lawyer and he needs to speak with you." She turned to the man. "If you'll excuse me, I will leave you to discuss your matter in private. Jaime, please show Mr. Standish out when you are finished."

Jaime nodded and pulled a green shirt over his head. "How can I help you?" he asked the man.

"Actually, I am here to help you, Jaime." He reached into his attaché case and pulled out a red folder. "I thought that you should be made aware of certain things going on around you."

"I don't understand," Jaime said, an uneasy feeling creeping up his spine. "Who are you?"

"That is not important, Jaime. What is important is that you find out this information, before it is too late—for you and for Mr. Race."

"Find out what?" he demanded, the sound of fear in his voice startling himself.

"Take a look at these photographs," the man said, giving the red folder to Jaime. "I believe that you will find them most interesting."

Jaime opened the folder to a photograph of Tim, bent over a naked Frederick van Nostrand. The following pictures were more of the same. Jaime rifled through them in disbelief, the pain of the betrayal beginning to sink in.

"Why are you showing these to me?" he asked, his voice choked with tears.

"There's more, unfortunately." He removed another folder from his leather case. "These are pictures of Mr. Race attempting to solicit sex from a male prostitute just last month at a location not far from here. As you can see from the photographs, the hustler in question is a young, thin Latino, not unlike yourself." He handed the folder to Jaime, who opened it up before closing it and allowing it to fall to the floor.

"Are you trying to hurt me?"

"Quite the opposite, really. I've uncovered a plot to blackmail Mr. Race for a large sum of money. This individual is very unscrupulous and powerful and plans to use this information as a weapon to hold over Mr. Race's head. You might not understand, but the movie-making industry is a bloodthirsty, cutthroat business. I'm sorry to say that your friend is going to be a casualty."

"What can I do to help Tim?" In spite of the damning photographic evidence, he still loved Tim and would never want to see him hurt.

"I think the best thing for you to do would be to leave this house immediately. I would go someplace far away, a location where you could lay low for a long while. You should break off all contact with Mr. Race. Continuing in a relationship with him would be very risky. They already know about you. You are in jeopardy if you remain here. Do you have a safe place to go?" he inquired.

Jaime tried to organize his scattered thoughts. "Yes, I think I do."

"Is it far away?"

"Very far."

"Good." The man reached into his pocket. "Here is some money for you. It isn't a great deal of cash, but I simply could not in good conscience let you leave without offering you at least a little money. Please, take this."

Jaime accepted the money. "Do I really have to leave here, now?"

"I'm afraid so, Jaime. It is much too dangerous for you to stay here. If the truth is exposed, Tim's career will be destroyed for good. You do not want that for him, do you?"

"No. I could never forgive myself if I did something to hurt his life in such a way."

"Again, I am sorry. I wish you good luck, wherever you go from here." The man then left Jaime alone in the bedroom.

"Why, Tim?" he cried. "Why was I not good enough for you?"

David arrived at Tim's Bel Air house at half past five in the afternoon. Mariana greeted him at the door.

"Hello, Mariana. Is Jaime around? I would like to speak with him."

Mariana wrung her hands in distress. "I am afraid not, Mr. Reardon. He came downstairs a little while ago with all of his things stuffed in a knapsack. He said he had to leave and that there was no time to explain. Then he took off in the nice car that Mr. Race gave him for his birthday."

"Did he say where he was going?"

"No, he did not. There was a man here earlier. He said that he worked for Mr. Race's lawyer and he needed some material from the house. I did not want to let him in at first, but I knew that Mr. Race would not want to be bothered after the death of his father, so I let him in. He said he also had to speak with Jaime and that it was very important. After this man—Mr. Standish—left, that's when Jaime came downstairs and told me he was leaving."

"I don't know of a Mr. Standish that works for Tim's lawyer. Did the man say anything else to you?"

"No, sir. Oh, *Dios mío,* I hope Mr. Race will not be angry with me!"

"Don't worry about a thing, Mariana. I'll take care of everything," David consoled, his mind trying to decipher what the implications of Jaime's sudden departure meant to Tim—and to himself as well.

★ 28

"I believe you should have this, son," Deanna said. She pulled a scrapbook with frayed edges from a dresser drawer in her bedroom. "I found this a few months ago. Apparently your father had been keeping it for some time."

Tim opened the book and inspected the first page. It was a clipping from the local newspaper about Tim's high school football team, which had made it to the state championship finals during his senior year. He touched the article lightly, the paper now brittle and yellow from the passage of time. Tim turned the page to find several photographs of him as a baby. In one photograph, his father was carrying him on his shoulders, both of them smiling for the camera.

"Daddy did this, all by himself?" Tim asked, amazed.

"Evidently. I didn't know anything about it until I stumbled upon it quite by accident. I thought that it would mean a great deal to you now."

There were clippings about his Emmy nomination for *The Drifting Clouds*; an ad for the local drive-in movie theater promoting *Death Never Waits*; a copy of *People* magazine with Tim on the cover, as well as several pages of photographs of Tim and Raina together. The last page in the scrapbook featured several articles and photographs about Tim's Oscar win for *Weak Are the Kind*.

"I can't believe Father kept this over the years. This means that he must have been proud of me, after all," Tim said.

Deanna wiped a tear from his cheek. "Yes, my son. I believe he was."

Raina knocked twice on the door before entering. "Sorry. Hope I'm not disturbing the two of you. I just thought Tim should know that we need to leave for the airport if we are to make our flight back to LA on time."

"Thank you, Raina," Deanna said warmly. "Your presence here has made all the difference in the world to my son and to me as well. I sincerely hope I will be seeing more of you both from now on."

"I promise you will, Mama. You can come out to Los Angeles and live with me, if you want to."

"Me, living in Hollywood?" she scoffed. "I don't think I belong there. That's your world, not mine. I wouldn't mind paying you a visit, however. And you know that you both are always more than welcome to come here anytime you want. It's not the kind of place you are accustomed to, but it's home, be it ever so humble."

"I love you, Mom," Tim whispered softly, hugging her tight in his arms. He had missed the feeling of being held in the arms by someone from his own family, someone with his blood flowing through her veins.

"You will always be my little boy," Deanna replied. "No matter what. There's no time for tears, now. The two of you skedaddle on to the airport before you miss your flight."

Tim paused at the screen door, taking stock of the house, which had changed so little since he was a boy. With his mother standing in the doorway to the kitchen, he saw himself as a child, running and playing as she stood over the stove, toiling over supper. He could almost hear his father returning home from a long day at the oil fields, sitting on a chair at the kitchen table and removing his dusty work boots. Those days were gone—gone forever. He truly *was* a grown-up now—in a big, often frightening world.

"Where could he be? He wouldn't have just left without saying a word, without telling me good-bye. That doesn't make any sense. Have you called his mother in Florida?" The desperation in Tim's voice was palpable.

"I spoke with both Lorena and Mario, and they claim not to know of his whereabouts," David answered. "Since he did take the Volkswagen, we can report the car stolen and have the police find him."

"And then haul him off to jail and send him back to Mexico in shackles and chains. Yeah, that's a great idea, David." Tim was inconsolable and snapping at everyone around him.

"David is only trying to help, Tim," Ruth said. "We all realize that you are upset, but snapping at us is not going to bring Jaime back to you."

"I just don't understand what is going on here. First my father dies, and then I return home to find that Jaime has taken off. And I want to know who this Barry Standish individual is and what he had to talk with Jaime about. You said that Derek Jacoby does not have a Barry Standish in his employ, correct?"

"I just spoke with Derek a while ago and he has never heard of this person," Ruth said.

"I should fire Mariana for letting some stranger into my home. This sounds like some kind of setup to me. Maybe this man works for the press and was threatening to blackmail me, which frightened Jaime off. When will we be able to view the security tapes? I want to see what this Barry Standish looks like."

"We should be able to view the tapes within the next several hours. In the meantime, I can call an acquaintance of mine with the LAPD and he can put the Volkswagen's license plate number in the computer and see if anything comes up. If the car is found abandoned or is involved in an accident or traffic infraction, it will show up on the computer."

Tim smiled at David. "Thank you."

"Don't mention it. I'll go make those phone calls now." David turned to leave the room.

Ruth stood behind Tim and put her arms around his neck. "Things are going to work out, Tim. You have to believe that in your heart."

"If he's gone, I never told him how much he truly meant to me. He's changed the way I think and feel about myself. I know I've made mistakes in the past—too many to count—but I was honestly trying to make things right with my Jaime—and with my life. I've been such a blind and stupid fool."

Raina appeared at the door. "What's going on?" she asked, immediately noticing the forlorn look on Tim and Ruth's faces. "Did something happen?"

Ruth answered for Tim. "It's Jaime. Apparently he's taken off without saying good-bye or telling anyone where he was going. Tim's a little upset, as you can tell."

Raina moved closer to Tim. "Talk about bad timing. I'm sorry, Tim. I'm sure Jaime will show up soon and everything will be okay."

"Do you really think so, Raina?" Tim asked, a glimmer of hope in his eyes.

"Of course I do, sweetheart. Everything will turn out just as it was meant to be."

"I just received a call from my friend down at the LAPD. There's been a blip on the computer database regarding the license plate number to Jaime's Volkswagen." David had rushed over to Tim's house as soon as his connection had called him, wanting to deliver the news in person.

"Oh, God. Please don't tell me that Jaime is dead," Tim prayed.

"Please, calm down, Tim. Apparently, the vehicle has been abandoned. Several tickets have been issued, and if the car is not removed within twenty-four hours, the police will impound it."

"Where's the car?"

"The car was left abandoned in San Diego. In Balboa Park."

★ 29

Raina and David took turns driving a shell-shocked Tim to San Diego. Since they left just as rush hour was coming to an end, they made good time on the darkened roadways.

"Tell me that I haven't screwed things up yet again," Tim said as they approached the San Diego exit. The memories of the night he had arrived in San Diego that past summer and discovered Jaime in Balboa Park were vivid in his mind. He had needed someone so desperately that night—someone to help ease the pain and uncertainty he had been feeling for so long. And he had found comfort in Jaime, someone who was young and carefree and nonjudgmental. It was the perfect relationship at the perfect time, and he had done his level best to sabotage it.

When they arrived at the entrance to Balboa Park, they found a line of cars waiting to enter through the West Gate. A black-tie, $2,000-a-plate fundraiser was being held at the Timken Museum of Art within the park. The elite of San Diego were now on parade in their finest clothes, smiling for the flashing cameras of the local media.

They found the Volkswagen Beetle parked just off the Plaza de Panama. Tim gave the spare remote key to Raina, who unlocked the doors. David carefully removed the collection of traffic tickets from beneath the windshield wipers and tucked them in his jacket pocket. Tim opened the passenger-side door and sat down heavily in the front seat. Raina took the seat beside him.

A white envelope rested on the dashboard. Raina lifted it up and inspected it before handing it to Tim. "It's from Jaime."

Tim looked at her blankly for a few moments before taking the envelope. He recognized Jaime's writing on the front of the envelope; he had always thought Jaime had such pretty handwriting for a man. He studied the sharp angles of the capital *T* in his first name, which flowed smoothly into an *i* and then into a perfect trio of half-loops that formed the letter *m*.

With trepidation, he finally broke the seal of the envelope. Enclosed, he found a simple piece of white stationery on which Jaime had composed a letter:

> *Dearest Tim,*
>
> *I know that my leaving will be a surprise to you. It is a surprise for me as well. I do not want you to be sad or to worry about me. I am going to be fine. It would never have worked out between you and me. We are from such different worlds. I want to thank you for showing me so many things and for being so kind to me. There will never be anyone else in this world that I will love the way I love you. Please, do not question yourself about why I chose to leave. This is for the best. You will see. I am not angry with you, for I know that you are a good person with a good heart. You will find someone soon, someone worthy of your love and that you can be proud to be with. Don't try to find me, for my mind is made up. You are far better off without me. Please, be happy. That is my greatest wish for you. I will never forget how you helped my family and I will pray for you every day. Thank you for everything.*
>
> *Love always,*
> *Jaime*

Tim did not speak after he finished the letter. He sat quietly, staring straight ahead. Raina watched him with growing concern. "Tim, are you all right?"

"No," he cried, placing his face in his hands. "I have been such a fool, Raina. I chased him away, like I chase away everything good in my life."

"You haven't chased me away," she said tenderly. "You haven't chased David away either."

"Jaime's gone. Gone for good. And it's all my fault. He didn't deserve to be treated the way I treated him. He is a good, decent person. Too good for the likes of me."

"You're being too hard on yourself. Your relationship with Jaime could never have worked out. Deep down inside, you've known that all along," Raina said, holding Tim's hand.

Tim had no more words to say. He rested his head against Raina's shoulder and began to sob.

"Let's get him home," David said somberly from outside the car. "You take care of him, and I'll drive the Mercedes back to Los Angeles."

"Everything's going to be fine, Tim," Raina cooed comfortingly into Tim's ear. "You'll see, my love. Life always has a way of working out for the best. Trust me."

"So, I take it everything worked out perfectly for you?"

"Smooth as silk."

"Smooth certainly would be the word. That access code you gave me did the trick at the front gate. And the envelope with the name 'Barry Standish' written on it was right where you told me you had placed it. Tricking the maid was a simple task, and the wetback was easy enough to get rid of."

"What did you expect? I'm not a novice at this, you know. I trust the half-million dollars I gave you will be sufficient to keep your mouth shut."

"Absolutely, ma'am. I've already destroyed those photos you had me take of Tim Race and the hustler. You have all the negatives. Planting a video camera in Tim's trailer was a stroke of genius. Can't believe the guy screwed the balls off that macho Frederick van Nostrand! I always thought he was a man's man, if you know what I mean. I never would have taken him for a flamer, but I guess you never can tell these days."

"Well, that will remain our little secret. Is that perfectly understood?"

"Whatever you say, Miss Hawthorne. I plan on taking my new windfall and heading down Mexico way for some much-deserved R and R. Maybe find me a little Mexican cutie, like in that Jimmy Buffett song. I haven't had me a decent vacation in a long while. Are you planning a honeymoon trip anytime soon with your Mr. Race?" The man laughed at his own little joke.

"Don't laugh, Fred. You'd be surprised what a little tea and sympathy can accomplish. And if that doesn't work, I've got a purseload of special pills and aphrodisiacs to get the job done!" Raina exclaimed triumphantly into the phone.

Epilogue

Jaime's return to Mexico was not met with any fanfare. As he no longer had family in Guanajuato, he moved into his *Tía* Floracita's crowded apartment in the Coyoacan *barrio* of Mexico City. Floracita's eight children also lived in the tidy little apartment, along with her husband, Arturo. Even though Jaime had been a little boy the last time his aunt and uncle had seen him, they welcomed him with open arms and he was quickly accepted into their loving, close-knit family. He shared a small, cramped room with his four male cousins and slept on a tiny cot that was an inch too short for his long legs.

His aunt and her three eldest daughters went to work each day for a wealthy family that lived nearby in the affluent neighborhood of Lomas de Chapultepec. Arturo and his eldest son worked in a petrochemical plant on the north end of the city that spewed highly toxic fumes into the air. Jaime found employment selling newspapers and magazines from one of the city's abundant kiosks in the famous Zona Rosa district on the Paseo de la Reforma, the palm-tree-lined boulevard that cut a wide swathe directly through the heart of the enormous city. He would take the crowded but very efficient subway to and from work seven days a week, just one of a million faces lost in the roiling sea of humanity that was Mexico City.

Jaime thought every day of Tim and the brief life they had shared together. He still loved him, of course, and would probably love him for the rest of his life. Sometimes at night when he could hear the slight snores of his cousins and knew they were asleep, he would take out the lone photograph that he had of the two of them together and cradle it lovingly in the palms of his hands. It was the picture Mariana had taken at the party Tim had thrown for his nineteenth birthday. Tim was smiling broadly, the same smile that had graced the covers of countless magazines around the world, as he held Jaime from behind, his arms wrapped tightly around Jaime's chest and his chin resting on the top of his head. The memories of that special day flooded him with a bittersweet melancholy. He had been so happy that day. No one had ever given him a birthday party like that before. He had felt so at home in the Bel Air mansion, so at peace with himself. There was no fear of not having enough food to eat, no fear of having to live on the streets too terrified of what might happen in the night to sleep. He hadn't bothered to tell any of his family about Tim. They wouldn't have believed him anyway. Jaime would then put the treasured snapshot back into his wallet and allow the tears to lull him to sleep.

A few days before Christmas, fate decided to hand Jaime another unexpected gift. It was near dusk and he was just about to be relieved of his duties at the kiosk when a man approached him with a copy of *El Mundo* to purchase. He was an older man with a middle-age paunch, thinning hair, and an acne-scarred face. He tossed Jaime a few crumpled pesos and told him to keep the change for himself. After he thanked Jaime and turned to walk away, he suddenly backed up again. He stared at Jaime's face, taking in the beauty of it: the high cheekbones, the perfect nose, the wide-set, dark chocolate eyes with the long lashes that curled upward to almost touch the top of his brow.

Jaime stared back at the man, a little uncomfortable with the way the stranger was looking at him. It reminded him of the way the lecherous old men had leered at him during his days hustling in Balboa Park. He shivered at the memory of their fetid breath on his face, their cold, clammy hands violating his body.

"Excuse me," the man apologized. "I don't mean to stare. My name is Arquemides Zayala, and I cast for several of the shows that air on TierraVision. Are you familiar with it?" he asked.

Jaime nodded his head politely. Everyone had heard of TierraVision. It was one of the most popular television networks in the country. His *Tía* Floracita watched at least three of the channel's *novelas*, the Spanish-language soap operas, each night.

The man continued, "Good. I'm looking for some young people to be a part of a street gang for an upcoming story line on *Mas Dulce Que Azúcar*. I don't want to hire professional actors but rather young people such as yourself, who have experience with life on the streets, as it were."

Mas Dulce Que Azúcar, Jaime repeated in his mind: *Sweeter Than Sugar.* It was a wildly popular show and starred one of Mexico's most famous pop stars and actresses, Lupe Esmeralda. He had caught a few episodes at night with Floracita and his cousins.

"Are you asking me to be a part of the show?" Jaime asked in an astonished voice, the twinkling lights from the Christmas decorations strewn across the Paseo turning the color of his hair to red and green.

"If you would be interested," the man replied.

What followed was the stuff of dreams, paralleling the plotline of one of the rags-to-riches *novelas.* Within days of their meeting, Arquemides had taken Jaime to the cavernous studios of TierraVision, where the television soap operas, talk shows, and game shows watched by millions of people throughout Latin America were created. He got to meet the beautiful Lupe Esmeralda, who had been so kind, gracious, and friendly to him. The first scene Jaime shot was taped in Chapultepec Park, the green lungs of a city caught in the unyielding stranglehold of dense smog and pollution. He didn't have any lines, but the camera caught his face and people noticed. A few days later, Jaime's character was added to the canvas of the show. He possessed a natural talent and looked handsome and at ease on camera.

Weeks later, when the episodes he had taped were finally broadcast, Floracita and Arturo were so excited and proud. Their own nephew, acting on a *novela!* Jaime felt as if he had achieved something on his own in life. Unlike American soap operas, the *novelas* ran for only a short period of time, usually between six months to a year. After the show ended its run, Arque cast him in another show he had created, this time with Jaime in a role central to the story. He had moved out of his aunt's apartment and was now living in Arque's beautiful mansion in San Angel, a neighborhood with quaint, cobblestone streets and full of historic colonial homes with wrought-iron gates and balconies. He did not love Arquemides, but he was treated wonderfully by him and he never wanted for anything. What Jaime truly wanted was the freedom to love whomever he wanted and to live where he chose, free of restraints. He would save up the money he was earning from work and would one day have the things in life that until now he had to rely on someone else to provide. He would think of Tim often and hold the precious memories close to his heart. Whenever he caught a commercial on television promoting one of Tim's latest movies or saw his beautiful face peering at him from the glossy cover of a magazine, he would pause and remember. At night, he would light a candle of benediction and pray to the sainted Virgin of Guadalupe that Tim was happy in the life he had chosen. He would offer a small prayer for himself as well.

Tim Race and Raina Hawthorne were married in a lavish ceremony on the island of Kauai on a brilliant July day. It had been an impetuous decision on both of their parts to get married, but a decision that made complete and total sense.

In the days and weeks after his father's death and Jaime's sudden departure, Tim had time to reflect on his life and the direction it was taking. He could not change who he was fundamentally, and maybe he would never be able to find the happiness in life he was searching for so madly. He had played the Hollywood game for too long. The road he had taken had been laid out before him stone by stone and he had just followed, blindly searching for fame and fortune. When he had reached what he thought was the end of the road, he was crestfallen to discover that it had only led him in an endless circle, and he was at the starting line yet again.

On the night Jaime left, he had turned to the one friend who could offer him solace: kind and wonderful Raina. He truly loved Raina, loved everything about her, from the twinkle of her eyes to the gentle lilt in her voice and the ease with which she smiled. He had felt so empty after Jaime left, and it was comforting to fall into Raina's familiar arms, to have her cradle him softly as she would an infant and to kiss his face and tell him that everything was going to be fine.

They made love that night, and it actually felt genuine to Tim. They had tested the waters before, of course, but Tim had found the water too cold for his liking. This time, however, the temperature was perfect. They sat on the bed together afterward, holding each other for hours, both shedding tears for what had been wasted.

When Raina told him she was pregnant, it was an answer to a question he had neglected to ask. The answer stood before him, and he bent down to kiss the stomach that would soon be round and distended from the life forming inside, a life he had helped create, as incredible as the thought seemed. Of course, they would be married. He would buy her a flawless twelve-carat diamond engagement ring at Cartier and they would invite the crème de la crème of Hollywood high society to the wedding. They would be the embodiment of the Hollywood power couple, inconceivably beautiful, living a life together in the Bel Air mansion that most people could only fantasize about. They would be married, and all the gossip and innuendo regarding Tim's private life would come to an end. He was going to be a father, after all.

David had been sad when they told him the news together. He had pretended to be happy for their benefit, of course. He had smiled, but not quick enough to hide the flash of sadness that fell across his face for a brief second. The feelings were still there, just beneath the surface. Tim knew that he would love David always, just as he would love Jaime. They both occupied a special place in his heart that would always belong to them and no one else.

All the major media covered the wedding. David had "leaked" the date and location of the event to the press. The wedding was to take place a week before the much-delayed LA premiere of *A Mission from Hell.* Rumors had already circulated that Raina was pregnant, and the two were met by a phalanx of rabid reporters upon their arrival at Kauai's Lihue Airport. They settled into their luxurious suite at the Sheraton Kauai Resort on gorgeous Poipu Beach. A ridiculously expensive wedding coordinator flown in from Beverly Hills mapped out their nuptials in exquisite detail.

While Raina busied herself with creating the dream wedding, Tim donned sunglasses and a baseball cap to cruise the hotel's magnificent pool. The lifeguard on duty caught his attention immediately. He was a native of the island, with deeply tanned skin, a lean but very muscular physique that was free of body hair, and full, luscious lips. From a distance, he reminded Tim of Jaime. He chatted him up and invited him back to his suite. The lifeguard had accepted the invitation with a brilliant white smile. Raina was still with the wedding planner at the chapel where the ceremony was to be held the following day. In his mind, he felt a slight twinge of guilt at what he was doing. It was just a part of who he was, like the color of his eyes and the shape of his jaw. It was the only thing he knew. Raina would understand and accept it; in the end, what choice did she have?

The wedding was held at an outdoor chapel overlooking the beach, on the grounds of a former Catholic mission and leper colony. Helicopters buzzed overhead and photographers camped on the beach and surrounded the chapel like an army readying to advance on an unsuspecting target. The wedding was officiated by a kahuna, a Hawaiian priest. Raina looked breathtakingly beautiful in her pristine white Vera Wang gown with the flowing train and bridal veil. Raina's parents had flown in from New Zealand and beamed with great pride from their seats beside a misty-eyed Ruth, so happy to see their beloved daughter on her wedding day. Tim had asked his old friend Talbot Grayson to stand up for him as best man, a duty he accepted with honor. An elite group of Hollywood dignitaries was also in attendance, among them David, who choked back tears in the last row of white, wicker chairs that had been arranged in the shape of a heart. The wedding planner had assured them it would look stunning when photographed from above by the daring paparazzi.

The reception was held at the resort. Dom Perignon champagne flowed from a crystal fountain, and the guests were treated to nouvelle cuisine prepared by the five-star chef from the Plaza Hotel in New York. It had been the perfect wedding. Tim knew the gloriously happy couple would make the covers of *People* and *US Weekly* as well as every tabloid and newspaper in the free world. All of the publicity would ensure *A Mission from Hell* a momentous opening weekend at the box office. Raina had a new movie coming out in a month's time, which would also benefit from the ensuing media frenzy.

At the end of the evening, when most of the guests were more than a little drunk and overstuffed on the limitless amount of food, Tim had a quick moment to himself. Raina was having yet more photographs taken with the wedding party. Tim slipped away from the crowd for a moment and went to stare at the beautiful ocean, spread out like black velvet in the bright moonlight. Outside by the pool was the set of intricately carved ice sculptures that had been created by one of the world's most talented artists, a disagreeable little man they had flown in—at great expense—from a tiny village in the South of France. The sculptures were of the golden couple and had been carved from a block of ice cut from a glacier imported from Greenland. They had posed together for the man several weeks before in California so he could sketch them in preparation for carving the sculptures. He had charged them a small fortune, but David insisted that this was the sort of thing expected at a celebrity wedding, something flashy and vulgar with just the slightest hint of elegance.

The statues had melted under the blazing Kauai sun, and their faces were distorted and no longer recognizable. From the reception hall, he could hear laughter and the clinking of glasses. It suddenly dawned on him that the ice sculptures were the ultimate metaphor for life. They were all ice sculptures, really: Tim, Jaime, Raina, and David. Beautiful, intricately designed, fragile, and fleeting—time would one day reduce them all to a shallow puddle of water in the unrelenting sun. As Tim stared at the figures, what had been the head of his likeness suddenly broke free from the sculpture and fell to the ground with a dull *thud*.

Tim released a sigh of resignation as he turned away from the sculptures and walked back to the party. Inside, his new bride was entertaining the guests with her beatific smile, her face aglow with happiness and from the tiny life now growing inside of her.

What more could any man ever hope for? he asked himself wistfully before returning to the reception hall and to the new life that awaited him there.

ABOUT THE AUTHOR

Michael D. Craig is the best-selling author of several works of nonfiction, including *The Totally Awesome 80s Pop Music Trivia Book* and *Who's That Girl? The Ultimate Madonna Trivia Book.* A longtime student of popular culture and trends, he also authors an online gossip column, The Retro Dish with Michael D. Craig. *The Ice Sculptures* is his first novel. He currently divides his time between Charleston, South Carolina, and San Miguel de Allende, Mexico, and is writing a new work of fiction.